INSOMNI

Alberts Bels is one of Latvia's most celebrated authors. With numerous novels and short story collections to his credit, his work continues to influence Latvian literature. Starting his writing career during a period when Soviet censorship was all-pervasive and Socialist Realism was deemed to be the only acceptable style, he was able to create novels that examined Soviet life and the psychological inner workings of individuals. One of his early books, entitled *The Cage*, which was published to great acclaim and translated into several languages, has since become a cult classic in Latvia. Other notable works written during the period include the novel *Voice of the Herald* and *People in Boats*. His later work delves into Latvia's more distant historical past, as well as the changes brought to Latvia after re-independence in the 1990s.

His many awards include an Order of the Three Stars, the highest civilian award given in Latvia, and a Lifetime Achievement Award at the 2012 Latvian Literature Awards for his oeuvre.

Jayde Will is a writer and literary translator working from several languages, including Latvian, Lithuanian, and Estonian. Recent translations include Artis Ostups's poetry collection *Gestures* (Ugly Duckling Presse), Ričardas Gavelis's novel *Memoirs of a Life Cut Short* (Vagabond Voices), and Arvis Viguls's poetry collection *They* (Valley Press). His articles, essays, short stories, and poetry have been published in *Words Without Borders*, *In Other Words*, *Lituanus*, *Panel Magazine*, and *satori.lv*.

INSOMNIA

Alberts Bels

Translated from the Latvian
by Jayde Will

Latvia 100

Latvijas Rakstnieku savienība

Kultūras ministrija

CYNGOR LLYFRAU CYMRU
BOOKS COUNCIL of WALES

Parthian, Cardigan SA43 1ED
www.parthianbooks.com
Supported by the Ministry of Culture for the Republic of Latvia and
the Latvian Writers Union
Insomnia first published as *Bezmiegs* in 1987 (censored), 2003 (uncensored)
First published in 2020
This edition published in 2020
© Alberts Bels 2020
© This translation by Jayde Will
ISBN 978-1-912109-42-5
Editor: Carly Holmes
Cover design: Emily Courdelle
Printed by Pulsio
A cataloguing record for this book is available from the British Library.

Translator's introduction

Latvian writer Alberts Bels's second novel *Insomnia* was written in the late 1960s, a time when the Soviet literary world was tightly controlled through censorship or the complete banning of work that was deemed to be hostile to the Soviet system. Bels's first short stories and his debut novel *The Investigator* received rave reviews for their innovative form and crime novel elements, but that soon changed with his following novel *Insomnia*, where he began to delve deeper into the mind of the individual in the Soviet system, directly representing life as it was being lived, and indirectly what was wrong with the system.

The official ideology of Soviet literature was Socialist Realism, which demanded that Soviet protagonists and the communist system depict reality, but that this reality be shown in a positive light. *Insomnia* touched upon several issues that were taboo at the time, such as a budding consumer culture that made people a slave to products, the housing problem that forced people to live in humiliating conditions in communal flats, and moral degradation in the form of things like alcoholism and prostitution.

The fragmentary and non-linear nature of the novel – small vignette-like chapters and interweaving plots that dart from 1960s Soviet Riga to the Nazi occupation of Latvia in the early 1940s, as well as the 12th century when the Brothers of the Sword were attempting to Christianise the Baltic tribes – was designed in part to throw censors off the scent of what he was really alluding to, which was that society was broken, and that the Soviet occupation was the cause. This and many other aspects of the book soon drew ire from the Soviet censors.

The initial manuscript of *Insomnia* was rejected by *Flag*, the leading Latvian literary magazine of the time in Latvia, as well as Zvaigzne, the country's most well-known publishing house. Through a twist of fate, the manuscript soon ended up in the hands of the KGB, and what followed were accusations of the book being anti-Soviet, and threats to the lives of Bels and his family. The book was never officially banned, but also never given a blessing to be published, one of the few books in the Soviet period to suffer such a fate.

It was not until almost twenty years later, in 1987, that a censored version saw the light of day. In 2003, the text was restored and finally published in its intended form.

Much in the spirit of novels of the time, such as Milan Kundera's *The Unbearable Lightness of Being* or Bohumil Hrabal's *Too Loud a Solitude*, Bels shows how people simply tried to survive by being, living in a parallel world in their mind, which was the only place they could live freely.

Though Alberts Bels is well-known and widely read in Latvia, and has been recognised for his work with numerous prizes, including a Latvian Literature Lifetime Achievement Award in 2013, his work is little known abroad, with the first and to date only English translation of his work, *The Cage*, published in 1990. It is hoped that this translation of Bels's genre-defying work can be a building block in creating a space for his work to finally take its rightful place among the greats of world literature.

Jayde Will, Riga, 2019

The Order of Events

My second novel *Insomnia* was written in 1967 and submitted at the editorial office of the Latvian literary journal *Flag* in February 1968. I had worked much with the form in order to make the composition of the book less linear. I used elements of modern prose in the composing of the text. It seemed that at the time *Insomnia* could have been viewed as a fresh development in terms of its content. However, the manuscript was rejected. Latvia's literary landscape had been ground down substantially by rumour mills, and word quickly spread that *Insomnia* was rejected due to some sort of heretical passages. In 1968 and 1969 I was studying in higher educational courses for scriptwriters in Moscow, which is why my communication with editorial offices in Riga was sporadic. It was only in January 1969 that I submitted the manuscript to the literary journal *Star*. But to no avail. Unfortunately a mole in the editorial office of *Flag* had dug deep and alerted officials in the Central Committee and the KGB responsible for such matters, because in one episode of the novel the name Noviks is used as an archetype, who was an old hand of the KGB protected by USSR law.[1] When I submitted the manuscript to the state publishing house Liesma in August 1970, I was met by stern warnings that it would be rejected, skipping any sort of procedure. (No discussion or review took place, as was stated by law.)

Clearly a decision had been made to give me a good licking.

In July 1970 I was invited to a meeting by two émigré Latvians,

---

[1] Alfons Noviks (1908-1996) was the director of the KGB of the Latvian SSR from 1940 to 1953.

a husband and wife, who were visiting their relatives in Riga. I went together with my wife to the meeting near Bastejkalns Hill, and we decided we would be as cautious as possible in our conversation with them. Another person, a relative of the visitors, came with them. For a short moment. But our surnames were mentioned. After exchanging a few pleasantries, the relative left. The émigré woman was pleasant, but asked questions nonstop. It looked like an unannounced interview, which is why I scrutinised every one of my answers carefully. Suddenly she showed an interest in the *Insomnia* manuscript. She had supposedly heard that I had an unpublishable manuscript. Why was it unpublishable? Well, no one was publishing it apparently. I said that someone would publish it. It often happens that it goes through five editorial offices without being published, but the sixth one publishes it. She asked if I had ever thought about a first edition abroad. I said that I had not thought of that at all. Could you give it to me to read? she asked. I said that once they published it, I would give it to her.

But the manuscript was already in their hands. They were just playing a game of cat and mouse with me. The afore-mentioned relative, using her connections with one of my colleagues, to whom I had given *Insomnia* to read, had taken the manuscript, read it, admitted it was a good book and, being an active and ardent opponent of the occupational regime, quickly undertook action. As a result, the manuscript did not end up abroad, but with the KGB. As it later turned out, the KGB had carefully followed all the activities of the married couple and their female relative. Thus it transpired that the formal reason for them examining the manuscript so closely were Latvian freedom fighters, who had carried out their work led by noble ideas.[2.] It seems they had

---

[2.] A reference to the afore-mentioned émigré couple and their relative. In many cases, the assistance that émigrés wanted to extend to their compatriots in the USSR led to problems precisely for the people they wanted to help.

forgotten to tell me one small detail (which was that the manuscript was moving around unhindered), so without a care in the world I, along with my wife, left for the forests of western Latvia, where I wrote *The Cage*, my third novel, near a lake in seclusion.

When I returned to Riga at the end of August, there was already a summons awaiting me in my flat that stated I was to appear in due haste at the KGB. On the 24th of August a copy of the *Insomnia* manuscript was placed in front me in an office at the KGB. 'Is this yours?' I was asked. 'It's mine.' 'Did you meet with émigrés, so they could deliver the manuscript abroad? How many copies did you give them to rewrite and distribute to the typist, whom you met with at the same time?'

Not a word was asked at the meeting about the novel's contents. There were only two topics under debate, which were my supposed wish to deliver the novel abroad and the involvement of the typist. If the operational officers had hoped to weave a thick net, it soon turned out that neither of those versions were credible. The conversation with the émigré visitors took place legally, and there was nothing of a secret manner either in the questions or the answers. Also, there was nothing criminal in the fact that I was introduced to the visitors' relative.

While reading the criminal case file in December 2000, I saw that the émigré visitor had understood the situation well (she had already been interrogated on the 6th of August). Our testimonies could not be used against one another, or against a third party.

Later, in the autumn of 1970, I was interrogated four times at the prosecutor's office. The tale of the novel being taken as contraband or it being rewritten for distribution was not mentioned. Only the contents of the novel. Investigator for Particularly Serious Cases, Eižens Kakītis, considered at least twelve episodes in the manuscript as anti-state.

The most interesting thing was that credible reasons for criticising the manuscript – the usage of Noviks as a prototype for one of the characters and the characterisation of the occupation, where one could make out contours of the Russian occupation in the portrayal of the German occupation – were not mentioned once.

I based my own defence on the dogmas of Soviet propaganda, the positions of the Communist Party congress and quotes from Lenin's works about the National Question. It seemed that I was successful in fending off all the arguments.

By that time I already had solid literary backing.

In the autumn of 1970 when I was interrogated at the prosecutor's office, the Moscow-based publishing house Khudozhestvennaya Literatura published the Russian translation of my novel *The Investigator*, and one of the most well-known literary critics in the USSR, Anatolii Bocharov, had written a glowing introduction for it. A print run of one hundred thousand copies was sold in four hours. The same year *The Investigator* was published in Lithuanian in Vilnius, and in Czech in Prague. It was in March 1971 that the literary journal *Star* began publishing *The Cage* right as a group of experts convened a meeting in order to compose a crushing blow about *Insomnia*. *Star* was a force to be reckoned with, and the print run was more than one hundred thousand. Their editorial office estimated that it was read by half a million people. It was spectacular publicity.

In April 1971 I read the corrections on the galley proof for *The Cage* and didn't suspect at all that clouds were once again gathering over my head. I was not informed about the initiation of criminal proceedings. Only God knows how my fate would have turned if Aleksanders Drīzulis hadn't been in the post of ideological secretary of the Latvian Communist Party Central Committee. He called me and told me without any sort of introduction: 'I have heard that you have some troubles with a manuscript. Give it to me to read.' I brought the manuscript of *Insomnia* over to him and a few days later I was invited for a discussion. 'The book is good!' said Drīzulis. 'But it can't be printed. The higher ups are against it.'

After some time, on 18th June 1971, I was summoned to appear at the prosecutor's office. Two KGB officers behaving as respectfully as English gentlemen acquainted me with the news about the termination of criminal proceedings. Of course, there was not a word about the true reasons for its termination. It was not said 'because Drīzulis barked at us!' or 'because the experts botched their job!' or 'this drivel isn't worth our time' or 'because the author fails to admit his true thoughts about the Soviet state' or 'an unpleasant debate about the crimes of Stalinists could arise in court and that in Moscow they will decide that the leaders of the Republic are unable to cope with governing' or 'because it isn't an anti-Soviet novel at all, but a cry for freedom and justice'.

Insomnia was banned neither openly nor officially. The officers that interrogated me behaved in a proper manner and played the role of civilised police officers.

In the middle of the summer of 1971, it was uncivilised police officers that came and sat down at a table in Līgo Café, where I was having lunch. The older one was over fifty, and the younger one around thirty. The younger one was a real gorilla, tall, wide shoulders, menacing. Only the older one spoke. He explained to me in no uncertain terms how my life would end and what would happen to my family if I ever attempted to publish the anti-Soviet work with the title of *Insomnia*. When I asked if they had been Noviks's stooges, he showed me his KGB officer identity card, signed by KGB Director General Longins Avdjukevičs.

The KGB had the bite of a bull terrier. A stable zone of silence was created around *Insomnia*, which worked perfectly both in Latvia, as well as abroad, until the beginning of Gorbachev's perestroika, when it was possible to publish an incomplete version of the book in 1986. Only now, twelve years after the 4th of May 1990 and thirty-five years after the writing of the novel, an opportunity arose for me to publish the text as it was submitted for publication in February 1968.

My case was Criminal Case No. 51356, which was initiated at the prosecutor's office of the Latvian SSR on 15th April 1971 according to the elements of a criminal offence stipulated in Article 1831 of the Criminal Code of the Latvian SSR, which is still stored at the Division for Supervision of Pre-trial Investigation within the Prosecutor General's Office of Latvia. It was only in December 2000 that I was able to have a closer look at the case and get the text of the expert group's opinion, thus acquiring proof that such a case even existed.

Alberts Bels
28 March 2002, Riga

Conclusion of the Expert Commission
Concerning A. Bels's Novel *Insomnia*

We, the undersigned, the expert commission in the following composition: Professor of the Faculty of Philology of the P. Stučka Latvian State University and Doctor of Philological Sciences – KRAULIŅŠ Kārlis, son of Jānis, Director of the Department of Party History of the Riga Polytechnic Institute, associate professor, and candidate of historical sciences HIMELREIHS Ludis, son of Pēteris, Senior Lecturer of the Department of Scientific Communism of the Riga Polytechnic Institute ĶILIS Arvīds, son of Jānis, and Director of the Latvian SSR General Directorate for the Protection of State Secrets in the Press RAMUTE Vilma, daughter of Kārlis, on the grounds of the decision of 9 March 1971 by the Latvian SSR Prosecution Office Investigator of Especially Serious Cases Com. KAĶĪTIS regarding the carrying out of the commission's legal literary scientific investigation – carried out a literary scientific investigation of the novel *Insomnia* by Alberts Bels over the period from 10 March 1971 to 15 April, 1971 and concluded that A. Bels's novel *Insomnia* is not written in a realistic style, but a modern one, using allegorical and symbolistic expression, shaping the characters established with a subtext of rather varied interpretations. Achieving a fully adequate understanding of the book is also encumbered by the fact that the author has not developed the work to completion in an artistic sense, which is why the novel contains numerous ambiguities, and in many cases it is impossible to find logically understandable answers to the questions that are touched upon.

In general we must say, that in Bels's novel *Insomnia* there are no artistically-portrayed characters, just a few phrases, which often are stated in the form of nightmares or gossip.

The novel *Insomnia*, even if we do not take into account its anti-Soviet mood and stance, possesses no artistic quality of any kind. In reality it is not a novel, but a pamphlet hostile towards Soviet rule.

However, the ambiguities in A. Bels's novel *Insomnia* are not so great that it would be impossible to provide answers to the questions of the Prosecution Office of the Latvian SSR.

The opinion of the Literary-Scientific Expert Commission

1. In A. Bels's novel *Insomnia* it is intended to portray life in Latvia under the conditions of Soviet rule, in other words our days. This is proved by the fact that on p. 56[3.] it is said, that the main protagonist Edgars DĀRZIŅŠ' childhood friend, who is a Hitlerite soldier Hansis, who falls as the German army is retreating from Latvian territory, has already been lying 'with the spirits' for 20 years (so the event takes place around 1964). The novel's protagonist Edgars DĀRZIŅŠ after the Great Patriotic War stays in the countryside for a time and works on a collective farm (p. 50). Also p. 94 and p. 95 tells about the developing of the collective farm's centre into farms (undoubtedly, with irony and sarcasm). What is more, in the novel there is a conversation about how already for more than twenty years careerists in the Latvian art world have been glorifying Soviet rule (p. 85), and many other examples.

2. The content of A. Bels's *Insomnia* is certainly ideologically harmful, because in it the Soviet state and societal order is slandered and disparaged, where both their foundations as well as separate aspects of Soviet life are mocked.

The novel *Insomnia* is saturated with an open and insolent tone from beginning to end. Thus, on p. 26 of the novel, the author states the following:

[3.] The numeration of the pages of the original manuscript were used in the opinion of the expert commission.

'In all lands, regardless of the societal order, the prisons are full, murderers and criminals rule nations…'

On the same p. 26 and also p. 27 with leaving for a time, allegedly, to be alone – 'within my four walls', the author made the following conclusion:

'Between my four walls I can feel like an absolute ruler. I can dare to hang any sort of picture with an orangutan on it on the wall and worship it, burning essential oils before it. I can dare to dance the most dreadful dances naked and boil my fellow countrymen in a cauldron. I can dare to demolish any economic and political system…'

Further on the author expresses that he could do nothing and sleep, but '…I need to reawaken, I need to reawaken, because otherwise I will live my life just as empty, as I have lived it up till now, and I won't have an excuse.' (p. 27).

With open mocking about Soviet rule, the following is stated on p. 85 of the novel:

'The exhibition was boring. Gray. Pale. There was just one theme in a few variations that was in play – ah, how good we have it finally, finally we have Soviet rule. And then they drone on, our loving rule, that longed-for rule, like for a girl.'

This and other anti-Soviet attacks on the foundations of the socialist order, and its derision are used by the author in many other places. For instance, on p. 127 – '…our social incubator worked at full force…'. The author targets in particular the essence of 'freedom' without making any sort of difference between that which is bourgeois and that which is socialist in some places. The following is said on p. 100:

'What is freedom actually? A word. This word will be banned in every land. If someone writes 'Let Freedom Live!' on the wall, they will be sent to the gallows at once...'

Whereas on p. 57 the author once again attacks the socialist society, just this time that we eat everything up and that is why we must take our last things to the pawn shop, and once again – '...freedom, you can't eat, otherwise we'd start on that too.'

3. In his novel, Alberts Bels scoffs at the Soviet people, their achievements in building communism, the moral and political maturity of the Soviet person is slandered, often even openly ridicules him disrespectfully, which once again shows the novel's anti-Soviet nature. On pp. 39-40 of this novel it is written:

'I am the best person in the world, the richest, the most socially insured... I can be treated at a polyclinic for free (... I know very well, that I already paid for it earlier, as I was healthy).

...I live in a resolute family of brothers, I together with my other brothers are united by a set of interests and goals, I am a tireless city worker, I carry the flag of socialist competition held high, I have a long-term goal – communism, I hold to the course of the victorious October, look, that's how I am, the statistical average. That's how I look at myself from the pages of magazines, from the columns of articles and reports... I am a superman. I am the best. I am the mightiest. Soon I will roar like a diesel engine, I will stomp the ground like an elephant, I will streak by like a supersonic fighter jet. Why do I need to clothe myself, eat, love? Why? I am so mighty. Let me be clothed, fed, loved! I, a person that's roaring, a person that can pat himself on the back, a person that's winning, a person going somewhere!

I have all possible freedoms, the freedom of gathering, the freedom of speech, the freedom of the press, I have all possible rights, the right to work, the right to holidays, I have everything, the only thing that falls to me is to produce, produce and once again produce, what falls to me is to become the very richest, the most cosmic, what falls to me is to simply produce.

I am a great cast iron founder and biggest caster of lies in the world… I have milked more milk, laid more eggs, hatched more chicks. But am I passionate about it? Are those numbers beckoning me forward?

At least I can be open with myself, I can admit the fears to myself…'

4. The author often strongly ridicules socialist labour. The topic of work is interweaved throughout the entire novel with an anti-Soviet point of view. Thus, the oldest daughter of Dračūns, the neighbour of the novel's protagonist, who works in a factory of the Latvian SSR, is compared to a 'Soviet slave, a workhorse.' The author writes:

'…Dračūns's older daughter worked in a factory at the stamping press, she pushed a worktable pedal more than one thousand times during the day with her right leg, which is why she slept like a rock at night, and the blood vessels of her right leg showed up on her skin like a strange, secret pattern, Dračūns's older daughter was a true Soviet slave, a workhorse, who pulled the state into communism…' (p. 84)

Whereas on pp. 62 and 63 the work of a Soviet person is interpreted only as production, as the decay of a person's spiritual strength. On p. 63 and p. 64 the Soviet state and society is shown as a mechanical work machine, which demands only that they work:

'I must work. I must work. No question' (p. 63)

    '...the state had received my work, but would then also take the flesh of my flesh?' (p. 63)

On p. 28 the protagonist of the novel says:

'Work, I told myself, work, that sounds horrible. When I even just imagined work, I trembled in fear. Work! It sounds absurd. Work had been turned into some sort of cult, some sort of perversion. Everyone is occupied with the glorification of work everywhere and most of all those, who themselves don't do a damn thing, from every wall of my home the invitation to work stares at me, an invitation to beat my head against work, although my brains splatter against the wall. I turn on the television, the newscaster shouts right in my face – work, you bastard!'

On p. 105 the novel's protagonist DĀRZIŅŠ in his inner monologue, in other words in a conversation with himself, speaks about the fact that we 'sell work, buy things,' ... 'we sell our arms, legs, brains, we sell our time ...we sell our desire, our nerves, we sell our health, we buy things... because the more things we'll have, the sunnier our future will be, we must produce, we must hurry to buy more, to sell, to wait, to wait, when finally we will be swimming in prosperity, carpets, cars, champagnes' ... 'everything mixes together, everything changes, owners become things, things before owners, we toppled the tsar and God, we raise up things, things...'

Here one of the most characteristic tendencies of A. Bels's novel can be clearly observed: to degrade the Soviet person, show him as a slave of things, who wants only to acclimatise, strives only for material well-being, but disparages a spiritual culture.

5. What rings throughout A. Bels's novel *Insomnia*, with a greater or lesser emphasis, is the thought about the discreditation of workers of Soviet institutions, where they are shown as ignoramuses, devoid of feeling, who are interested only in that a person works, would be a thing, an obedient screw ('because only then is their rule iron-clad, if no one sticks their nose in the door of those in command.') (p. 97).

This discreditation is clearly manifested, when the author depicts the life of a morally lost girl and her stay at the Riga Railway Station.

'The militia would check documents every hour, asking the traditional question 'Where are you travelling?' the slow-witted officers not understanding that she wasn't travelling anywhere. She wanted to sleep at night in a waiting area meant for passengers travelling long distances… however the railway gods and militia gods came at midnight, checking the documents of each that found themselves in this paradise, where it reeked of sausages, rye bread and foreign people…' (pp. 17-18)

6. From what is cited in numerous places written by A. Bels and other examples, one must make the conclusion, that the author scoffs at the friendship of Soviet nations, and propagates bourgeois nationalist, anti-communist views. For instance, the aforementioned concept 'foreign nations' that was emphasised on p. 18, as well as the broad irony on pp. 39-40 ('I live in a resolute family of brothers, I together with my other brothers are united by a set of interests and goals…').

In order to show that the Latvian youth is nationally-minded and propagates anti-Semitic ideas, and is against Communism, the author describes a gathering of former schoolmates, involving the use of spirituous liquids, in the following way:

'…and the merriment came out in full force, and the song 'Here, where the pine forests sway.' …

'Then Jānis suddenly belted out 'Merry Boys Are Shooting Jews on the Shores of the Gauja Again!' and everyone laughed… he continued singing 'there's only one gun, but a whole slew of Jews!' and Valters shouted 'throw the Jews in the fire,' almost all of us were Komsomol Youth, but no one told him to stop, everyone was drunk, laughing, some sang along, and then Valters once again shouted 'Jews and communists in the fire!'… 'Yes, communists in the fire, are there any communists here?' It seemed like a joke to everyone, and those, who saw that he was serious, pretended not to hear him, and he seriously shouted it, it was all so wonderfully merry there, I had no intention of standing up, I wasn't even a Komsomol Youth, maybe I was going to make a horrible scene, but those novices were going too far, I got up and yelled 'I am a communist!' and Valters howled… pointing at me with his finger he spilled cognac on and saying 'moron!' (pp. 86-87)

7. After the aforementioned account about A. Bels's novel *Insomnia* one must make the following conclusion, that Soviet rule is not cherished by the Latvian nation, that an entire class of Communist Youth are nationally-minded, that Soviet rule in Latvia is bound with a 'foreign nation', that Soviet rule has turned the Latvian nation into a 'work horse', into a thing, that the nation is broken, that it is not in their interests anymore.

Without a doubt, the novel *Insomnia* in its metaphorical and literal sense sounds like an anti-Soviet work, which could be understood as an invitation to fight against Soviet rule.

Professor of the Faculty of Philology of the
P. Stučka Latvian State University, Doctor
of Philological Sciences   (K. KRAULIŅŠ)

Director of the Department of Party History
of the Riga Polytechnic Institute,
Associate professor,
Candidate of Historical Sciences (L. HIMELREIHS)

Senior Lecturer of the Department
of Scientific Communism
of the Riga Polytechnic Institute   (A. ĶĪLIS)

Director of the Latvian SSR
General Directorate for the Protection
of State Secrets in the Press   (V. RAMUTE)

INSOMNIA

Midnight

1

Sitting in a deep, worn-out lounge chair, in which Mr. Dārziņš had so gladly sprawled out back in the old days, I was reading a book and smoking a pipe with pleasant-smelling tobacco. Although low temperatures had persisted for a few nights, the window facing the street was open, and my legs were pleasantly warmed by a soft camel-hair blanket. The hands of the enormous clock, the first a short, fat man just like Sancho Panza, the second a tall, slender man exactly like Don Quixote, were approaching midnight.

Having put down the book on my lap and suddenly having forgotten the sentence I had just read, I listened to the sharp, nervous steps on the street. The pointy clopping heels clicking closer and closer, the knocking on the asphalt reminding one of the rhythm of telegraph keys, I clearly heard fear and bewilderment. The clock rang out slowly and uncannily.

Having gone to the window, I saw a woman running from the direction of the lake. After a few steps she looked back. Turning her head and shoulders, the slender figure in a grey, nylon raincoat froze for a moment, then ran on ahead once again. It looked like she wanted to hide herself in a building or courtyard. It wasn't hard to understand that, as her entire behaviour bore witness to this; besides, insomnia had sharpened my senses.

She pulled on the gates. They were closed. She ran further on again and then ended up next to Jauniks's building. It was there that she also stopped for a moment.

She couldn't hide in Jauniks's courtyard. First and foremost

1

because the courtyard was surrounded by a fence made of high boards, with two lines of barbed wire two and a half metres off the ground surrounding it like a defence battalion of prickly hedgehogs. The gates were closed shut, and a terrifying dog called Koba lay in the yard. An angry and uncontrollable beast. People would witness as Jauniks walked around, hitting his dog with a six-tailed whip, and only then did Koba give in, yelping and howling pitifully, and two or three beads of sweat would drip from his master's brow onto the dog's shiny combed back. Then you understood that hitting his own dog after it ran after a bitch passing by was a difficult job, an unpleasant job.

Jauniks was a strange and secretive man. I didn't know where he had come from, where he had arrived from, what he occupied himself with. He was retired, and, upon seeing him for the first time, an inexplicable disquiet inhabited my soul, as if I had met a person who possessed a great secret inside himself. Jauniks was a handsome, stocky sixty-five-year-old or so gentleman of average height, yes, really, a true gentleman (the only thing that didn't fit with his appearance was perhaps the dog whip), impeccably dressed, with perfect manners, a smooth gait. This quiet and taciturn man disappeared behind the high fence of his private home. The cultivated garden, apple trees, plum trees, gooseberry bushes, and lilacs were very much visible from my window. No one knew anything at all about Jauniks. Even Mrs. Grīzkalniete would throw up her hands if asked, saying she didn't want to talk about it, and that meant something. It was said he had a bad liver, a dismal past, a hopeless future; to tell the truth it didn't interest me much at all, what did I care about all these rumours, gossip, and tittle-tattle of women?

The woman stood near Jauniks's house for a moment. One could understand she was thinking of whether to run on further or try to pull the gates open. Having looked over the fence with barbed wire around it, she ran further on, and I was wondering why I didn't hear the barking and growling of the dog. This time the dog was nowhere to be seen. I quickly looked toward the far end of the street, however I didn't see her pursuers. When the woman was more or less opposite my window, I yelled:

'Hello!'

She jumped, rushed to the side of the street, stopped and looked up.

'What happened?' I asked. 'Was there an accident?'

'Yes,' she replied.

'Can I help you?'

She didn't reply, but opened the gate, went through the small garden and stopped at the front door. It was locked. I threw the key down, which clinked several times as it skipped to a halt on the footpath. A minute later the woman entered the house. I stepped out into the corridor and opened the door to the stairwell. She was standing right in front of me.

She was approximately twenty-five years old; the corners of her mouth had settled into a expression characteristic for pessimists and she had dark bags under her eyes, most likely smeared eyeliner. Her clothes were wrinkled.

It was dark in the corridor, which is why I couldn't make out anything else. From the opened door of my room, a little path of light stretched over the carpet. Without saying a word, the woman went along this path into the room and at once went over to the window. Leaning a little over the windowsill, she looked towards the lake, then turned around and leaned with her back against the windowsill as if waiting for me to say something. The glass of the open window threw a reflection from the lamp onto her cheek, a sliver of light fell on her temples, and during that first moment I thought that the lamp had moved, but then I realised that the woman was clinging to her last ounce of strength so she wouldn't collapse on the floor. Her eyes closed, but I was already there, and caught her in my arms and took her to the couch.

Though my knowledge of medical matters is rather poor, I could say with certainty that she had not fainted: the deep, regular breathing, the expression of extreme peace on her face, and the strong, normal pulse bore witness to the fact that the woman was in a deep sleep. I found a pillow for her, put it under her head and fluffed it up, and after thinking about it for a moment, removed the woman's coat. She didn't wake up. She didn't wake up a moment later either, when the entire building was jarred by a chilling scream.

Midnight

2

Our building sounded like a violin.

Wood, splinters, plaster, paint, two storeys, eight families in two flats. Asters's room was located right next to mine, its wall was protruding out like the edge of an octagonal redoubt with a glass-encased embrasure. Asters's nervous system often played such tricks on him: heart-rending screams rang out in the night, all the windows would light up, only the culprit continued to sleep soundly; he didn't even wake up from his own screaming. Asters treated his nerves with music. He was always a quiet person, he walked through the hallway inaudibly like some spirit or troll from a Scandinavian fairy tale, he treated his nerves with music, and that is why they dubbed him the 'waltz driller'. He was of tall stature, blond and wiry, with a wide mouth, and lips thin as a frog's. When I had to go away on business, and in recent years I had to go away on business more and more often, I packed my suitcase with a sigh of relief; in the foreign, distant cities my ears were not worn down by his sweet waltz turns. Regardless of whether I returned from the Urals, or from Leningrad, or from Tbilisi, I was cut into pieces again and again by that circular saw of the waltz. It was so quiet on the street Sunday mornings that you could hear how in Asters's room the curtain string was sliding through the reel, while the curtain itself, lightly rustling, slid up, and soon after a real waltz could be heard. Once I counted how many needles he had used, how many records he had worn out in the span of a year, how much he had damaged my nerves in treating his own. Asters continued to spitefully play his records on his old gramophone that perhaps was from Biblical times. In the end I developed a kind of maniacal necessity to listen to these waltzes. If it happened that I spent more than a month on a business trip, I began to miss our street, the fine clay strip of bluish asphalt with a slope down towards the lake. I began to miss Asters's waltzes.

At home I also had to wait, a few mornings a week, for at least forty minutes before I was able to use the bathroom and toilet room. Of course, I should duly admit, that it's just because of my carelessness or, to be more precise, inertia that I ended up living in such uncomfortable conditions. I had attained a certain status in society, my name was one to be reckoned with, I had worked my way up from a rank and file economist to an authoritative scientist and the work gave me the appropriate means to purchase a large and spacious flat. However, the bohemian slumbering deep within me wouldn't let financial concerns burden him, or, most likely, it was me who decided that it was not worth losing time and energy busying myself with the improvement of my life. My spiritual nourishment came from the economic bulletins of the more developed countries, the estimates and projections of industrial equipment; I devoured all of it in an unbelievable quantity and speed. Thanks to everything from my natural talent to a phenomenally well-trained memory, at the age of thirty-one I was able to achieve a level, which a rare few achieve only at sixty years of age.

Everything in my small room was designed for work comfort. Next to the side wall was a large couch as long as it was wide (now the unknown girl was lying down on it fast asleep), two wardrobes and linen closets were built into the wall, then a three-level bookshelf (I should say I had collected a rather substantial library), and, finally, a compact TV and radio unit squeezed into the corner. There was no more than eight square metres of free space left.

So I lived in that building, in reality right in the lair of hell, to say nothing more.

Five families dwelled in the five rooms on the ground floor. In the big room, right under me, lived the liqueur factory taster Dračūns with his wife and two daughters. As for Dračūns, he was a man of short stature with an intelligent face, always dressed in grey attire with a repulsive blue tie on a checkered shirt, always stooping, as if in addition to his flesh and bones he was carrying sixty kilogrammes of lead on his shoulders. Already from the beginning of getting to know one another, Dračūns himself provoked interest with his open and unreserved opposition. He criticised the government in all questions. If Dračūns was given a megaphone and allowed to participate in an election campaign, he would shout in a boisterous voice on the street that 'all deputies have sold out their revolutionary principles.'

'What?' Dračūns said. 'Sanitary living space? Of course I have it, four point five square metres for each family member, which is why I am not taken into the queue for flats. A horse in a stall has more space allocated to it. But I will have to live in this cage my whole life! And if I want a work room for myself, a guest room, a separate room for each of my daughters? What then? What should I do? I have to take a loan of two thousand five hundred roubles, wait a few years in the line of the co-op. What is two years, a thirtieth of our lives? But, comrades, are we going to spend our whole life like this? Our entire life is then just standing in a queue. And then I will be in debt up to my ears, I will slave away giving it back right up to the edge of my grave, what the devil do I need all that for!'

Later I learned that Dračūns had a lover, who lived in the city centre. I have to admit, I was surprised. It turned out, this fact was also known by Dračūns's wife, however she always acted like she was neither worried nor affected by it. Later I learned that actually this fact affected his wife more deeply than I could have imagined. His wife weighed ninety-five kilogrammes, and just as weighty and inevitable was her decision to give away both of her daughters to a man at the right time. Of course, not to the same one, it was preferable for each daughter to have their own husband. Without a doubt, the girls could still await the festive moment, the older one was nineteen, the younger one just sixteen, so the girls could still have awaited the moment they go out into the world, but the cup of patience of both parents, in particular that of the mother, was full. Women are always more sensitive to domestic comfort or discomfort, and now I should say, living on the ground floor was an enormous act of bravery, to put it mildly. Five families used one bathroom (without hot water), one toilet, five families had one kitchen, no more, no less than fourteen square metres big, with five portable cooking stoves there, smelling of fish boiled in petrol, and during breakfast, lunch and dinner five mothers, each eighteen times more quarrelsome than the hen of a brood, boiled, fried, stewed, made dumplings and argued about the living space. Dračūns's wife had earned the honour of being the most quarrelsome woman of the building, and the remaining four kitchen dwellers united in a joint front against her. Dračūns's wife dreamed of the moment when a noble son-in-law would take their daughter away, no matter which one, and allocate a small, proper little room in his flat for his mother-in-law, where a woman stranded in life could relax from the traumas acquired in the communal kitchen, as well as from the scenes, which were forever orchestrated by her husband, the small liqueur factory taster. If Dračūns's wife could find a trustworthy female friend, to whom she could entrust her secrets of the heart down to its most hidden chambers, then this girlfriend would find out that in reality this wife was very hurt by her husband's buzzing around his centrally-dwelling lover, that that was why she quarrelled in this kitchen of five witches, that the last drop in this cup of agony had fallen last week, when Dračūns had notified her with 'farewell forever', tucked the gramophone under his arm and with his hat slightly aslant on his head disappeared in the direction of the centre. With his hat slightly aslant on his head! That just showed that the vile, swinish feelings in Dračūns had gained the upper hand over the sweet, sensitive family man he still was, yes, still, despite all the scandals, he was. The worst thing was that three days later Dračūns returned with his gramophone, the device was broken and Dračūns's wife found out that his lover supposedly had just a small room in a communal flat and in that central building it was apparently just as much of a mess as in the outskirts, and, as he was sitting on the only toilet, there were already five renters pacing along the hallway, gritting their teeth in anger, holding their trousers in their hands, and poor Dračūns apparently couldn't handle it. What parallels! It was only because of that he returned, and not entirely out of pure-minded love for his portly wife. What misfortune! Mrs. Dračūns had silently dreamed that finally she had gotten out from that cheating litmus test (which is what she called her husband when no one heard her), however the litmus test repented for his sins, disclosed his paths to darkness (as well as his lover's address), and his wife went to curse about the broken gramophone, but his lover turned out to be the same kind of portly woman beaten down by life without an ounce of ill-naturedness in her soul, and then both of the unhappy women cried to their heart's content, over how bad their husband and lover was.

'He doesn't even know how to repair a gramophone,' his lover sobbed.

'At least he doesn't drink!' Dračūns's wife said, refuting the allegation.

Dračūns didn't drink because he didn't dare ruin his refined taste-tester palate, but that also was the only bright spot in his thoroughly dark life. After a three-hour conversation both women came to an agreement, that Dračūns was the following:

'All he is is a litmus test (with a small 'l')!'

'We will have to bear this cross to the end of our days!'

'The hardest are the laundry days, because there's just one bathtub.'

'There's worse husbands.'

But in the fights, and the fights took place often, when the four kitchen queens joined together in a united front against Mrs. Dračūns, Dračūns always helped his wife. The beginning of the fight was foreshadowed by a flood of words. The squabble bubbled slowly, as if accommodating, as if flowing, and you could hear all of it wonderfully in the first-floor kitchen near the ventilation shaft, because the air flow shaft was shared for both kitchens. You couldn't make out individual words, but as a result they seemed all the more weighty. The stream shimmered, moved and began to flow faster, then something like thumping intruded in the monotonous murmur of voices, a saucepan or frying pan rattled on the stovetop more strongly than usual. Then at one moment they seemed to quiet down, hesitate, and the rustling turned into a low-pitch effervescence; it all reminded one of a swirling river near mill locks. Someone threw the lock open, saying the last, unforgivable sharp word, as the saucepans struck one another like shields, and then it started, what a fight it was! Mrs. Dračūns held her own against their superiority valiantly, so her voice resounded like a fine, forlorn trumpet, calling the cavalry for help. Dračūns, jumping quickly to his feet, rushing from their room, where he had already been listening at the door for a long time, waiting for the right moment and preparing himself inside for his difficult mission. And I saw with my own eyes how easily and energetically he invaded the kitchen, because once it happened that I entered the ground floor hallway right at the moment when the escalated conflict had struck its final chord. Flapping like pancakes, slaps fell upon the cheeks in the kitchen, while one of the four allies sacrificed hot soup made out of chicken neck and leg broth in a small pot onto Dračūns's head, and Dračūns, enraged by this to a white heat, providing well-aimed strikes left and right with tightly-clenched fists, beat back the women's battalion out of the kitchen, while Mrs. Dračūns sobbed near the window, saying 'Oh, the horror, it burned me.' When something hot had been poured on Dračūns's head, he fought like a beast. The neighbour women disappeared into their rooms a moment later and Dračūns himself appeared in the hallway, casually pulling out the remains of the broth from his hair with a victor's hand and removing a small chicken drumstick stuck behind his ear.

Of course, if the women would unite in a joint front against Dračūns as well, they would gain the upper hand rather easily, however there was always some sort of tactical error that was allowed, which could be expressed in the short phrase 'They certainly couldn't have poured boiling broth on Dračūns's head.' While the broth boiler stated her claim to the broth pourer, Dračūns wriggled out alive and healthy, conquering his enemy piece by piece. There was just one time he had to dig deeper into his wallet and pay the lonely mother, Frosya, money for her pain. The house caretaker, Urka, compiled a bill, fining him three roubles for a bruise on a hidden part of the body and six roubles for a bruise on her face.

Urka, the house caretaker, was a true parliamentarian by nature. He didn't deal with any issue without long discussions and voting. I remember well one day last autumn, all the adult inhabitants of the building had gathered in the first-floor kitchen so they could discuss an important issue. The quarrel stretched for a good half-hour and, judging from the look of things, they hadn't approached some sort of solution. Not one of the renters wanted to undertake the difficult work on their own.

'Petya,' said Urka's wife Lyolya, 'we'll take out the toothbrushes, but not the magazines, newspapers, and book covers! Dračūns's girls collected them, so let them get rid of them. Petya, what did I tell you!'

Urka was Latvian, however he spoke accent-free Russian, and everyone only ever called him Petya. He had forgotten long ago that his name was Pēteris.

Dračūns said that he wasn't going to throw out the toothbrushes, so let someone else do it. The old newspapers, yes, he would do that, his girls apparently hadn't scattered them about, he had left them scattered about, which is why he would get rid of them, but the toothbrushes, empty shoe polish tins and book covers, those had supposedly been scattered about by Urka's son Jura, who was known around the entire neighbourhood as an infamous troublemaker, breaking windows with a slingshot and ripping books apart.

But one person could do it, we'll cast lots, I suggested. No! Alone? Why does one person have to take out all that crap? We can do it together. All of us together! But then someone yelled again, that he had not brought in the slightest of filth into the cellar, not even what was on the soles of his boots, because he always wiped his shoes, he wasn't going to take out someone else's piles of rubbish, if other people wanted to live like pigs, then he also wasn't going to cast lots, it would be moral capitulation! When I quietly got up and left, no one even noticed, they all just fervently strove to prove that the cellar needed to be cleaned immediately and right away, the heating season was right around the corner yes, yes, it needed to be cleaned, clean, clean! About twenty minutes later, when, after I finished cleaning that stupid little cellar, I returned, they were still in the same place they had started. When I said that the cellar had been cleaned, they stared at me like a ghost, as if I had come carrying my legs on my shoulders, everyone got up from their seat, and made a beeline downstairs to take a look at the miracle. After that they considered me a show-off and careerist and droned on about it for a couple of months. Whatever!

Urka's wife Lyolya worked in a roadside restaurant, while Urka was a plumber. He fixed the central heating boilers, radiators, drainpipes and many other things, which he didn't have the slightest clue about. He fixed Dračūns's gramophone, and after that the record spun in the opposite direction and all the music was played backwards, and Dračūns screams of 'The needle is broken!' resounded up to the first floor.

The afore-mentioned single mother, Frosya, still lived on the ground floor, and the rumourmongers gossiped that a holy spirit had been seen at her place quite often and that in the very near future she would be awaiting another child out of wedlock. In the corner room lived a grey-haired and universally respected widow. Seeing her on the street with a grey fox fur wrapped around her shoulders, one could never imagine that it was precisely her that had poured the broth made by Frosya on Dračūns's head. In the opposite corner room, to the north, lived a married couple with the last name Tomiņš, a harmonious family with two children.

Two of the first-floor rooms were occupied by Asters with his wife and their son, a student. Aunt Who Breaks Waves had settled in the small room. As a paramedic on a ship, she had once tried to explain to the children in the yard, what a wave breaker was. It turned out that a wave breaker was entirely different from a bone breaker, and that nickname stuck to the aunt like a mollusc on the submerged part of a ship. Currently Aunt Who Breaks Waves is situated far away in the Atlantic.

In the fifth room lived Grīzkalniete. It wasn't without pride she considered herself the neighbourhood's eyes and ears. If I know all the details of Mrs. Dračūns's visit to her husband's lover, then I have Grīzkalniete to thank for that. If I know that the holy spirit often visits Frosya, the lonely mother, then the holy spirit is depicted with Grīzkalniete's mouth.

Once upon a time Grīzkalniete had been young.

Young and beautiful, her favourite story was of some factory worker, a facial cream manufacturer, who looked for beautiful girls around all of Riga so one of the most beautiful ones could then be used in an advertisement photo on the cover of a cream container. The choice had fallen to Grīzkalniete (please forgive me, I'm trying my best to retell what I heard), however Grīzkalniete refused in true girlish pride, and did not grant him permission, because she supposedly had never used that cream in her life, though she had soft and white skin all the same.

Her other favourite tale was about her grandma. Once upon a time Grīzkalniete had had a grandma. Once upon a time that grandma had been young. The little girl dreamed about a yellow velvet dress – it could also be made from grey velvet, or also from red velvet, but definitely velvet – and she had wanted to get this dress as a gift on her birthday. Then year after year passed by, the little girl grew up, got married, gave birth to Grīzkalniete's mother, then Grīzkalniete also appeared in the world, but that little girl was now an old, old woman. Someone would always promise to gift her a grey, or red, or yellow, or green, or blue, or rose velvet dress on her birthday. The old woman died, and that dream never came to fruition, but, when they laid her in the coffin, they remembered that once upon a time there had been a dream, and decided to made her a black velvet funeral dress. But it turned out that everyone was busy with organising the funeral and didn't think of providing even one kopeck to pay a tailor. No one at home wanted to sew one either, and so it happened that the old woman was buried in a black silk funeral dress. What was there to worry about, they thought, she supposedly didn't have one while alive, so she didn't need one dead either. So now often a little girl comes in the depths of night to Grīzkalniete, asking for a yellow or red, or blue, or green, or rose-coloured dress.

Midnight

3

The more I looked at this unknown person sleeping, the clearer it became to me that she hadn't seen warm water for at least a week. Her neck and forehead were grey, a rather dirty layer of powder covered her cheeks, and her dark hair hung in greasy tufts. I bent down and took her shoes off, and I saw that the shoes were black from sweat and that her pantyhose was torn in several places. Her facial features were symmetrical and even beautiful, but didn't make up for the overall impression, and I understood how poor my judgment had been regarding this woman.

I decided to heat up the metal stove in the bath with some wood, warm up the water and tell her she should take a bath. Who cares if she is easy, why should she have to be dirty on top of all of it? I put on my leather jacket, took the keys and also my slippers without putting on my shoes, and went downstairs to the cellar. The firewood had been chopped long ago. I collected a good armful, and returned to the apartment. Ten minutes later the fire was going at full blast, the crackling flames raced into the air vent, with a yellow flame that could be seen blowing about through a crack in the stove. The water heated up in the basin, I turned off the tap, mixed twenty or so grammes of bath liquid in the water, and hung up my robe on the hook next to the bathtub. Since buying a new robe, this one had been kept in the wardrobe unused. Afterwards, I went to wake the unknown woman. I thought that it would take at least an hour before she would come around from her deep sleep, however it was enough to grip her firmly by the shoulder, say 'Get up' in a stern voice, and she opened her eyes right away.

'Go to the bathroom,' I said, 'and clean yourself up. I will just make the bed, and you can go back to sleep.'

She didn't ask anything, didn't protest one bit, but obediently got up and followed me. Like some sort of sleepwalker! At one moment I became uneasy, I began to have doubts whether or not I'd be able to figure out this woman correctly, but it was already too late to go back.

'You can lock the door with the hook,' I said, 'it's a communal apartment, someone could walk in on you. Look, here's the soap, there's a towel there. When you're done, put on that robe.'

She quickly began to undress. I closed the door, she fastened the hook, and I listened for a moment. Water splashed in the tub and then the woman made a sound like a big cat purring.

She was in the bath for a long time, but I didn't dare to return to the room. I was afraid that she might fall asleep in the tub and drown. I paced in my soft slippers from one end of the corridor to the other. Finally the water stopped splashing, the shower was turned on, and then I was certain that she would not fall asleep. I returned to my room, and put sheets and blankets on the couch.

When I went to the corridor, Asters, my neighbour, damn him, was trying to get the bathroom door open.

'Oh!' he said, surprised. 'I thought that it was you taking a bath in there.'

The unfortunate thing was that one could only get to the toilet room through the bathroom, and after that horrible screaming in the night, Asters suddenly had the pressing urge to make a lengthy visit to the toilet.

The little hook clicked in the bathroom, the door popped open, and I took a few steps back, breathless. Asters gaped in turn, and a broad smile slid across his face. The unknown woman stood totally naked in front of us, her clothes swinging above my striped robe on the hook. With a sleepwalker's expression on her face, she went past us, and into my room as surely as if it was her own. I heard the creaky springs of the couch and the rustling of the blanket. I would have never believed that a woman could walk so shamelessly naked through a stranger's apartment, but I had to experience that with my own eyes.

'And I thought it was Ulrika in there! But you already got another beauty!' said Asters. He burst out laughing so hard that his eyes narrowed into slits and his mouth stretched almost up to his ears. There was no doubt as to what he was thinking upon seeing this woman in her suit from the Garden of Eden coming out of the bath. It must be said, from what I managed to see in that short moment while she stood on the threshold, she had clearly been transformed after her bath. I have to admit, I had been mistaken in determining her age, this unknown girl could not have been more than nineteen or twenty years old. In turn, Asters had not been mistaken in calling her a beauty, as her body truly was worthy of admiration.

I didn't even think to explain anything to Asters, let the man fantasise about whatever he wants to fantasise. I returned to the room. The unknown girl was laying down, fast asleep. She could get up and fall asleep quickly, like an animal. Or do a marvellous job of looking like it. A person knows very well what he needs most at the present moment, which is why I decided not to disturb her sleep, or ask her anything until she had slept. You shouldn't ever force events; I bore that in mind. All I could do to help her was to let her sleep, even a child would have understood that. But then I had to think about her, about her nakedness under the blanket. She was so beautiful and so well-shaped, and so young, and blindly obedient. All kinds of thoughts thrust themselves upon me, that I could take her without any effort, in her half-sleep state she would give herself up to me anyway. I already wanted to undress and lie down beside her, however I didn't do that, but instead looked out the window.

An unknown girl was sleeping on my couch, I didn't know who she was, why she had entered my room, how long she was going to sleep, why she ran from the direction of the lake at night, who she was running from, why she so obediently fulfilled my orders, and another thousand and one whys. Why? In the end, why did I care? Perhaps she wasn't running? Perhaps she was walking in the late evening, struggling with her illusions? So why was I imagining all this? I know very well why I called to her, why I invited her up, why I told her to bathe, made the bed with clean sheets, what all of those unnecessary ponderings were for; some sort of phlegm of the conscience. Screw all of that!

Midnight

4

The time comes and a person finds out everything. I also found out.

She had spent several nights in a row at the station, in the waiting area for the shuttle buses, where a crosswind blew, where people walked non-stop, where the militia would check documents every hour, asking the traditional question 'Where are you travelling?'; the slow-witted officers not understanding that she wasn't travelling anywhere, that she didn't have anywhere to travel to. Where could she go? It didn't matter where, but she said a station, named some place in the provinces very far from Riga, some place the train left for only in the morning, and she was allowed to stay on a bench in the crosswind and hubbub, but under a roof and in warmth more or less. She dozed off and her head jerked back up periodically, as if praying to God, but her god was sleep; she dozed off and dreamt of sleep, she didn't dream anything big, no, only little things, she wanted little things: to sleep at night in a waiting area meant for passengers travelling long distances, where it was warm, instead of more or less warm, and the benches were soft, upholstered with fake leather. Each evening she tried to sneak into this area and stay the night, she almost managed to sneak in, however the railway gods and militia gods came at midnight, checking the documents of each person that found themselves in this paradise, where it reeked of sausages, rye bread and foreigners. While checking documents, they found that she shouldn't be there and chased her downstairs to a cold bench in an unheated area in a crosswind where they let her sleep, but she could only doze off sitting up. If she risked lying down on the bench, then a blue uniform would pull her to her feet during his next round because she was weak, but the militia officer was as vain as a peacock in his sense of his power, in his sense of his stupidity. There were also good militia, civilised blue-uniformed officers, a large majority of them world-wise men, who allowed her to sleep in the crosswind on the cold (more or less warm) bench the whole night, the whole night, right until morning, right until morning.

In the spring she found a building in Riga's Old Town and snuck into it with a trembling heart in the middle of the night. There was a bench in the stairwell on the first floor, but the first night she didn't dare lay down there. She listened, half-sitting, half-worried that someone might open the door downstairs, that someone might come to strangle her, to rape her, to ravage her, however nothing of the sort happened, just some tenant coming back late passing her in a rush and intoxicated daze without even noticing the lonely creature on the bench. That was even scarier. He didn't even see her. No one, no one, one, one. That entire big city was snoring away on their couches, in their beds, on their seaweed and spring beds, but she, Dina, had gotten very cold early in the morning, her clothes frozen through and through, she climbed up the stairs, and the gust of warm air coming from one of the apartments through a crack in the door, reminded her like a painful lash of the people sleeping in warmth, comfort, and slumber at night.

In the morning she went to the station, washed up in the bathroom, did her hair, had breakfast in the station buffet and went to work. She worked in a printing house as an assistant. Now and then in the evenings after work she would visit friends, and tried to stay long enough that they would offer to let her to stay the night, so then for one night she would feel happy. But it always happened that around three nights a week she didn't have a place to sleep. However, she was proud, didn't ask for help, thought it over, she wanted to hold out another month or so while she looked for a house for herself. She had been living like that for a couple of months already since two overweight, kind-hearted Latvians, a husband and wife, had kicked her out.

Late one night she was walking past the restaurant "Riga" and to a building in the old town, and a woman stopped her.

'Help me, help me get that animal home,' she asked.

The animal was standing on the sidewalk, slightly swaying, his legs spread out wide: stocky, content with himself and the whole world. The animal had the face of an honest and happy Average Joe. The animal appeared to be benevolently satisfied, like a well-fed pig, and didn't move from his spot.

'I am a robot,' he said. 'Tick, tock, tick, tock.'

The woman prodded him, pushed him, swore at him, pulled him along, almost spat on him, but the animal just carried on with his new role.

'I am a robot,' he said. 'Tick, tock, tick, tock!'

He appeared to be so immoveable that Dina understood strength would not be of any use in this case. To be honest, she didn't want to interfere at all, she wanted to go past them, also like the many that had gone past her, but curiosity took the upper hand. What would happen if she tried to turn the robot on, tick, tock, tick, tock, you Latvian, overweight shlub, you slave to your stomach, move, my dear man, tick, tock, tick, tock, you Latvian, maybe it will work, let's see what he does.

'Click!' Dina touched the man's shoulder, a shoulder dressed in a good coat. Under that good coat was, tick, tock, a jacket that was just as good, tick, tock, and a button-down shirt that was just as good.

'What?'

'Click! I turned you on. You are a robot, aren't you?'

'I'm a robot! Tick, tock, tick, tock!'

'Then you have to go! You're turned on.'

The humane, endlessly good-natured, honest, happy Joe, that overweight animal, swung around and suddenly came flying with a punch, trying to hit the woman that had asked Dina for help.

'Go away,' the man said to the woman, 'go away!'

The woman shrieked and sidestepped his punch.

'You can't do that,' Dina said.

'Pardon me! You probably pressed the wrong button. But I like you. You're not afraid of me?'

'No.'

'Well, then you are an honest person. I need an honest friend, I don't have one honest friend. Come with me, I will show you my boy, you see, I have a little tick, tock, a robot!'

And it was there Dina realised what she had only felt when she stopped: she was infinitely exhausted, endlessly tired, she had had enough; her pride powerless against the iron shaft of life. She'd go with this stocky, good-natured, honest Joe. She had had men thrust themselves on her with such offers both at the station and on the street, but they were just men, their appearance alone raised suspicion, but this man was an honest, good-natured tick-tock little robot. She'd go with him, she'd go just so she wouldn't have to go back and spend the night on a bench in a building in the Old Town, she'd go along. She had already felt when she stopped that this woman, this nightwalker from the restaurant, wasn't Dina's competition, and Dina saw that the fat, good-natured Joe understood that. One fat Latvian, two fat Latvians, three fat Latvians, long live the good-natured Latvians, long live those good-natured Latvians, long live the good-natured Latvians of all sorts, the short Latvians, the tall Latvians, the tick-tock little robots, the Latvians. Dina sat in the taxi together with that good-natured Joe, but the unhappy nightwalker, that stupid girl, who had brought her misfortune upon herself, remained on the street, clenching her fists and elegantly expressing her opinion about dishonest competition.

At home he had a lovely, small, sleepy little tick-tock robot, a little boy, one with a velvety nose; he was all alone, their villainous mother had left them both.

For you, pretty girl, you shouldn't have to waste away in some shitty printing house. Or do you think that sixty roubles is enough? You have a cute bum, and tits, and a small waist and a pretty face, and I, the little tick-tock robot, like you! What more do you want, stay here with me, live here as long as you want. Look, I'll kiss your little legs!

Dina stayed. Within a few months her character softened, she relaxed, she became so lazy that she didn't even protest when the fat, good-natured Joe said, blinking his eyes guiltily: You understand, you can't live at my place anymore, just some things have come up, don't get angry, but I got you a room at someone else's place. So I guess this is goodbye!

And he gave her fifty roubles. He was a good man. Dina went to live at the place of that 'someone else'; she already knew him a bit. While visiting the tick-tock little robot, that 'someone else' had often thrown eager glances Dina's way. She lived there about a month, then took her roubles, this time just thirty, and moved to the next 'someone else'. In this way she slid ever lower, she changed hands more and more often, and finally she happened upon a good girlfriend, who taught her the tricks of the trade, and who took care of the clients, and it was last night this girlfriend had happened upon a perfectly acceptable client for Dina, so she went with him, however the client turned out to be a sadist, a monster, a scumbag, and Dina was barely able to escape. The client had taken her to a small shed on a pier near the shore of the lake. Dina had ditched her bag and went into shock. 'Some would crap their pants at times like that,' she told me, 'but I fall dead asleep. I can sleep anywhere, even on the street, if I am frightened. It was so crazy,' she added.

I found all of this out in the morning, when Revolver Mike came and I was leaving to accompany her downstairs to the front door. Mike said that Dina changed men like hats, and then Dina also told me everything with a vindictive frankness, but for the time being I stood at the window, and an unknown girl slept on my couch, and all I knew was that I had let her in because my Ulrika might be far away in a foreign city at this very moment at night somewhere on the street looking for help. It could happen to anyone, fate is not blind then, fate is sharp-eyed, and that is why I needed to call out to that woman, warm up water in the bathtub, put on clean sheets, let her sleep, let her sleep, let her sleep, and not give a damn as to what my neighbours thought, what that unhappy nightmare-ridden Asters thought.

Midnight

5

To live means to enjoy. After all, why not? Even in something as inconsequential as walking across the street, I enjoy the roundness of the cobblestones under my feet, the earth's cheek, though masked, nestled up to my soles.

I believe that a person should take everything from life that comes to them, and even more; you need to rob life like a rich miser on a highway. A person comes into the world naked, but life dresses itself up in expensive furs, which is why you need to rob and plunder the rich misers as much as possible and the most beautiful things possible, for in the end everything will be taken away anyway. Robbing will turn out to be either a hilarious vaudeville act, or a bloody drama, and, as the curtain falls, the bills will have to be paid and you will have to return to ashes and dust, not as naked as you arrived in this world (because you will have received some decent rags after so many years of looting and plunder), though in reality you return in nothing more than a narrow and uncomfortable mode of transport.

I succeeded in happily combining the perception of a material life with successful studies, a happy relationship, a fulfilling daily routine, and, almost naturally, I began to wonder whether fate was preparing a trap for me, as had already happened seven hundred years ago or seven hundred and fifty years ago; indeed, I can't remember exactly, although my memory, as I have mentioned before, is otherwise faultless and to my knowledge phenomenal even.

Upon waking, I rejoiced in the day. I did the same concerning night while falling asleep. Going to work, I rejoiced in my work, and going home I did the same concerning my leisure time, and it was in that encompassing joy my life passed until the age of thirty. When I was young, everyone expected great things from me, they expected that when I was older I would become a part of their faction, camp, or what you could call a current, which formed in the community of every city, which is why it's no surprise that in this incubation period of one's personality, I didn't have enemies. I have to confess, I began to worry about it and, upon acquiring my first enemies, I was no less happy than when experiencing one's first ice cream in the sweltering heat of summer, or one's first swim in the sea, one's first slalom skis, one's first flight in a metal whale – an airplane. Like one's first long separation.

'I will write you a letter every day,' Ulrika said.

'Ulrika, dear, you won't have time.'

'At least a postcard. Two lovely words.'

'I don't expect you to write. You won't have time. During the day there will be rehearsals, meetings, guided tours, foreign cities. Shops as well. In the evening you'll have to perform, dance, you know very well yourself there won't be time.'

'I will write as often as I possibly can.'

'Alright.'

'Oh. We'll be going soon.'

I kissed Ulrika four times, five times, six times and then a seventh time, because there's a song that goes 'you kiss seven times'. Seven in general is a magical number. I am not really superstitious, which is why I kissed her an eighth time, and then the group leader couldn't stand it anymore, and literally pulled Ulrika from my embrace and pushed her into the train carriage. The train wheels clanged, the tracks groaned, the train shook and went forward. Where else if not forward?

Love is a complicated primer, we turn page after page, learning to recognise one new letter after another. It may happen that as you are turning a new page, the brilliance of your impressions will smother all those that came before. I turn to the page about distances. The packing of your luggage, the ache of departure on the platform, of course, carefully concealed, the varnished sides of the wagon, the red cap and disdainful face of the station master, because he can't go anywhere.

Midnight

6

My main principle is to not cling to anything too much. Let everything flow on past like clear, flowing water, let it run like a rabbit with light feet, then living isn't so hard. Up until now I've avoided marriage, that number one horrendous noose. I've avoided relatives, that danger number two. In fact, it was easiest for me to avoid danger number two, because I don't have a single living relative left. I am all by my lonesome self. Ulrika might be the only one I've gotten too attached to lately. Perhaps it's precisely because of that I was silently ecstatic about our separation. For more than a month I would once again be alone. No one, alone, only me?

I have been running away from social responsibilities like a devil from a cross. I have run away from aesthetics seminars, from various group activities, I have run away from communal work on Sunday, I have run away from collective visits to the theatre, I have run away from group tours, so in a sense my views are totally anti-social. More than anything I hate crowds, with crowds being any sort of larger group of people who don't have their own initiative, their own idea.

I quickly and ably got free of the crowd of those accompanying me, and with a nod of the head I said goodbye to my acquaintances. It was a miracle that Ulrika's parents had not come to see off their daughter. I understood it was most likely because they didn't want to meet me. They didn't have to. I could have chosen not to come. Ulrika's father and mother didn't exactly see me in a positive light; a deviant, a womaniser, those were the more relatively mild of the epithets they bestowed upon me. Ulrika dared to tell me those and we both had a good laugh. Of course, after going out with this young woman for two years, not expressing the slightest wish to be bound in matrimony, ignoring her parents' invitations to come and visit, it seemed in large part strange, to say the least. However, over the last months a strange tenderness bound me ever tighter to Ulrika; I even began to worry whether I was getting old. moreover Ulrika lived for three months at my place, in my tiny communal flat. The craziest thing was that I had begun to get used to it all. I didn't want her to become either my common-law wife or my lawful wife, however I didn't have the power to alter the balance of things, and now this trip came along as a saviour. Well, Ulrika's parents were probably right, I really was a cold person, an egoist, only reckoning with my whims and wishes; I didn't feel any sort of pangs of conscience. And what were pangs of conscience anyway? It was a feeling of guilt, the awareness that you hadn't done everything, so the world could be better, and people happier. But I can't fix the world. It seems to me that everything on earth is fine as it is – the oppressed are oppressed, the free are free, the happy are happy, the unhappy are not, and, as long as man lives, evil will also live, a few bright souls will forever stand up against evil, and the bonfire of Giordano Bruno will blaze eternally. I don't want to take part in this mess, I don't want to burn and I also don't want to bring the logs to the fire. It's enough for me to stand on the side and watch. I know history adequately enough for me to say that the masses, what is called humanity, cannot be set right. In all lands, regardless of the societal order, the prisons are full, murderers and criminals rule nations, so let it be. While I stand calmly, no one is grabbing me by the neck, and, as long as no one is grabbing me by my neck, I can stand calmly.

Between my own four walls I can feel like an absolute ruler. I am able to hang any sort of picture with an orangutan on it on the wall and worship it, burning essential oils before it. I am able to dance the most dreadful dances naked and boil my fellow countrymen in a cauldron. I am able to demolish any economic and political system. I am able to write tracts crammed full of humanism and addressed to those hundreds of years in the future – the citizens of the future. I am able to do nothing, lie quietly in my bed and die, die for eternity. Who knows why I want to be laid on my right side in the coffin, with both hands under my head, so I would be fast asleep, fast asleep, sleeping for millions of years, billions of years in my shanty of flesh, in my one-hundred-and-eighty-three-centimetre long and seventy-kilogramme heavy shanty of flesh, and so I would once again be fated after such long years to reawaken; I must reawaken, I must reawaken, because otherwise I will live my life just as empty as I have lived it up till now, and I won't have an excuse.

Between my four walls I can feel like a caged jaguar, I can gnaw at the iron bars of my cage and my teeth will become dull. I am able to growl in my impotent rage against my prison guards, and they can simply laugh at me. I can be a humane jaguar and not tear apart the white rabbit that they throw in as bait. I can eat nothing, lie quietly in the corner of my cage with lazily half-closed eyes and die, die for eternity, and my skin will be stuffed by an old and wise master and will be put on display with other jaguars as a warning.

Between my four walls I can feel like a human being, and that is the hardest, because I feel how I am loved.

In reality love is just a small lightbulb, a lightbulb of a tiny happiness in the dark night, in the night when the earth is cloaked in darkness and people are covered by loneliness, in the night the sky revolves around the earth like a giant barrel with a silver spigot, and someone who has grown up only with this barrel and has been fed solely through this spigot knows nothing of the outside world. Someone opens the spigot, black pitch begins to rain down, the black pitch will carry you away into a deep ice hole, lost in loneliness, a white lightning bolt flashes overhead, like a dog howling pitifully, in the night, as the earth is cloaked in darkness and people are cloaked in loneliness.

So why should I lock that reflection in a ring? Gold in and of itself is not evil, people have made gold a stumbling block. Gold is a noble metal, but I don't want, I definitely don't want to put love in a ring.

Midnight

7

After going on holiday I had sworn to myself to not think about work; I swore to not try to solve some problem connected with work. Throughout the year I was yoked to my work, though my heart hungered for rest. The world of numbers and iron logic is awfully dispiriting. Work, I told myself, work, that sounds horrible. When I even just imagined work, I trembled in fear. Work! It sounds absurd. Work had been turned into some sort of cult, some sort of perversion. Everyone is occupied with the glorification of work everywhere, and most of all those who themselves don't do a damn thing. From every wall of my home the invitation to work stares at me, an invitation to beat my head against work, although my brains splatter against the wall. I turn on the television, the newscaster shouts right in my face – work, you bastard! The moment is not far off anymore when they will start to glorify work on the wall of the men's room. Work? But after all, work is necessary for a person's life, something sacred, just as necessary as sleep, just as much as air. But do we glorify sleep? We will sleep, comrades, we will sleep strengthened, prolonging your life, snoring, lightly wheezing. We will sleep on couches, in nickel-plated beds, we will sleep on seaweed mattresses, foldable cots, in the worst case we will sleep in sleeping bags or on plank beds and, if there won't be anywhere at all to sleep, then in stations, haystacks or the drier foots of hills on the side of the road. We will sleep, comrades!

I have slept horribly the last few years, quite horribly, since I started thinking less about my career and my work, and since I began thinking more about life, about other people. I sleep horribly, quite horribly, but for the time being insomnia doesn't seem to be influencing my working abilities. At night, when sleep has escaped somewhere in space, I dream about a small airplane, which belongs to me alone. I could go flying for a few hours, make the most daring loops, ride above the very tops of the blue spruce forests of Dundaga or also zigzag along the Gauja River, the crazy river, so the edges of the wheels would be dunked in the water. However, that's all nonsense, I will never have an airplane; who will let me purchase a little tiny airplane for myself? My friend Pāvels Fjodorovičs told me:

'If you really want one, you could build a little plane lickety split.'

'How?'

'You see,' he continued, 'it's quite hard to obtain something through official channels, bureaucrats are sitting almost everywhere, and, if there aren't any respective sanctions then it's fine. But if you come to me at the factory not as an economist but, let's say, as a private person and say: 'Pāvels Fjodorovičs, I really need an airplane motor, couldn't you help me out, you know, we could drink some black balsam[4], and think of some options!'"

Who knows, maybe I really could find such a motor. But you would pour some black balsam and talk more.

'Pāvels Fjodorovičs, maybe you have a friend that would have, let's say, an airplane wing? Let's drink and think about it!'

Who knows, maybe I'd find such a friend, and with time and patience you'd have a little airplane, and you could go visit, well, you already know who, and say:

'Jan Janovičs (or how do you Latvians call one another, when you speak in your own language?), let's say, Jan Janovičs, couldn't you perhaps allocate me a little, tiny piece of airfield, because you see, I already have an airplane!

---

[4] A traditional herbal liqueur

And I'm telling you, it would fly like an angel, we could go for a ride!'

Pāvels Fjodorovičs had a point, and I gradually began to understand that it was just due to my lack of enterprise that I was sitting without an airplane, I began to understand that it was only due to my lack of enterprise I was not sleeping at night, dreaming about having a small, tiny airplane which I could use to fly back in time, seven hundred or seven hundred and fifty years in the past, then when I would start to touch down, I could see where my unlived life was left, my unvanquished struggle, where my great love was left, and slowly, slowly I remember everything, a horse is galloping, a trail of dust curling behind the riders and I think that everything will be ok, everything will turn out right.

The Witching Hour

1

Misfortune does not sleep either, and yesterday during the afternoon, when the forests all around Riga lay bulked up in the sweltering heat, the master returned to the castle. Galloping through the stream, a dapple horse suddenly tripped, the rider flew from his saddle, with water getting into his deerskin clothing under the silver armour, however the master didn't want to be late waiting for the clothes to dry as there was less than a four-hour journey left to the castle. The rider galloped, steaming in the afternoon sun, with a halo of buzzing horse-flies around his head. Quite unexpectedly he was held back at a checkpoint, the twilight surprised him, and the chilliness wrapped itself around his limbs. Today, when the envoy arrived, the master was lying down in the round room of the tower behind the thick granite walls with a cold, sneezing from time to time, and his servant placed hot stones wrapped in sheepskin that had been soaked in wine under his feet.

'Lord, there is a letter for you from the knight commander,' I said.

'Aha, give it here!'

The master tore open the red wax seal, and unrolled the yellowish parchment roll.

'Do you know of the contents of this letter?' he asked.

'Roughly, yes.'

'What are your thoughts on them?'

'I believe that the Order is not powerful enough to continue the construction of the church.'

'The power of the Order or lack thereof is well-known to me already. I am asking about the witchcraft!'

'I am certain that the Order is confronting a well-organised resistance.'

'Yes, witchcraft, unknown hands, the devil, the god of the pagans, that is all utter nonsense. If an evil spirit had gotten mixed up in this issue, why would he need to destroy walls at home with no one witnessing it? In the light of day it would act, in broad daylight, it would not just destroy what was built once, but scatter the stones around the area, so no remnants are left near the building site. The knight commander is a fool, he believes in his own invented illusions. Of course, the people, the dark masses, that sort of mysticism is all they need. Who makes the food for the guards?'

'A trusted person.'

'I am asking – who?'

'Someone from Bremen, thirty years of age, a contract worker.'

'What kind of weaknesses does this Bremenite have? Does he love money, beautiful women?'

'I have no obligation to know such a thing.'

'A good viceroy needs to know everything. The Bremenite could be bought off. Nothing is easier than to add some herbs in the wine of a sentry. Arrest the Bremenite at once, interrogate him, and if he doesn't confess, torture him with a hot iron. You knew everything, you understood it, why did you not tell the knight commander this?'

'Evian Steele does not believe in the truth, if my tongue expresses it.'

'I will order him to believe. But his idea? You are aware of the knight commander's idea; what do you think of it?'

'I think that it is folly. It will enrage people unnecessarily. It will cause unrest.'

The master was lounging around on an inclined flat oak

triclinium, a man of rather short stature, a true machine of muscles and tendons, a twelfth-century warrior, a ruthless man and good rider, and harsh in implementing his decisions. He sat up, and the servant placed a bearskin on the master's shoulders.

'I want that you understand me,' the master said. 'I want that you would steer public opinion in my desired direction in an intelligent and discreet manner. I believe in you and want to explain why I am taking such a decision. It is clear to every sensible person that it is not the god of the pagans that is involved in this, but rather the people, and the people must be assuaged by the sword. Why rob a beautiful pagan girl of her life? It would be more proper to dispatch a division of the Brothers of the Sword and stop the unrest in one fell swoop. However, having carefully weighed all of the pros and cons, I have come to the conclusion that we could use the idea of the knight commander Evian Steele. We will spread rumours that we believe in the mischief of the pagans' god and only because of that will wall in a girl so the wall would become sacrosanct. At the same time the bought-off Bremenite will have to be eliminated, the guard will not lose sleep at night, the temple of worship will stand as it has been standing, and, in effect only a few people will know the truth, and we will have gained an important ideological victory. Our god will have vanquished the pagans' god. Of course, this plan would not be adopted if I had a sufficient amount of soldiers at my disposal in order to keep all the lands subjugated, in order to punish insurgents at once, but at present I don't have many men and swords, the Order is far away from their bases. I cannot plunge myself into a serious battle, which is why I must operate with cunning in the hope that they will believe in my words, believe in the Order's military might, because only the truly strong are able to act in a ruthless and merciless way. My diplomatic experience bears witness to the fact that this trick works. Essentially, I have no other choice, as otherwise we will have to suspend the construction of the church. What's more, the Order's primary focus will be side-tracked, but we cannot show the Latvians that we are wavering on even one point. You see, I am open with you.'

I was silent. The master's openness frightened me.

'If this plan turns out well,' the master continued, 'we will give you the opportunity to see the world. To travel. Visit holy sites. Hopefully, even the pope will give you an audience. You will see faith in all its might.'

'Rome?'

'Rome.'

'Such a journey is expensive.'

'The Order will take care of it.'

The servant handed the parchment to the master, then gave him ink in an ivory vessel.

Dark premonitions crept into my soul. When I was appointed to my post, I thought that I could at least partially lessen my people's misery, at least partially ward off the black clouds. As a viceroy, I knew the situation in the land well, I knew the true extent of their might. With a united resistance we could crush the Order, but internal quarrels, self-aggrandising, and distrust year after year weakened our might. Our conquerors cunningly took advantage of each mistake. I had observed them carefully for a long time, I had studied the highest-ranking supreme commanding master's weaknesses and deficiencies in his style of rule. Knowing that he loved quick and bold answers, I tried to speak in a language that was open almost to the point of extremes, giving the impression that I was not hiding anything and fully trusted him. I was almost always in opposition, however, concerning trivial matters I always deferred to him, openly admitting that the Order's interests were higher than anything for me. Once I confessed to the master as if in passing that I was placing all my hopes on the future when, together with the Order, I will rise to never-before-seen heights above my people, that individual personal sympathies mean nothing to me in comparison to the great sympathy, the Order, that I have bound my fate forever with the Brothers, just with the Order, the Order, the Order. Give me the Order, and I will give you my people in return. So I was successful in creating the illusion to my master that I am a power-hungry individual, a complete sell-out, a thinking man's realpolitik politician, sharp and unamiable for sure, but entirely faithful to the Order.

I was leading a double life. At the same entirely in secret I was uniting forces, readying a revolt. I looked for Lithuanian allies, I looked for Estonian allies, but at the present moment the Lithuanians were pummelling the lands of the Russians, while the Estonians were roaming and pillaging Vidzeme up in the north, so we had to rely solely upon our own abilities. We could begin the revolt no earlier than in autumn of next year.

For some of the more hot-headed, the church built by the Order and the heavy corvée tied to it was a thorn in their side, and my efforts to smother the conflict at its roots was not successful. Now a premature armed clash was threatening. The master was also leading a double life, his spies were not sleeping; now I understood what trap I was caught in, there was no clearer evidence than a regiment of riders, two knights, ten brothers, and fifty soldiers that had appeared in the courtyard. They would take me to the Commandry. Just a few minutes before the master had stated insincerely that he supposedly didn't have the forces, that he, only forced by his lack of might, supposedly wanted to wall in a girl, and now his treacherous plan was as clear as day. Of course, the people would not tolerate such cruel mocking, the swords will become unsheathed earlier than expected, blood will be spilled, victory will smile upon the Order, potential rivals will be eliminated. I will also have to show my cards. I didn't truly trust my gut feelings yet. The master was applying a seal to a letter. I felt that he was hesitating, I felt that he was waiting for yet one more question from me, and for a moment I was afraid to ask him. However, it was dangerous to stay silent any longer.

'Does the master know who the girl will be?'

'Yes,' the master quickly replied. He really had been waiting for precisely this question, and my heart became clenched when he looked at the commander's letter. 'Evian Steele writes that it will be one Ulrika, an unbaptised heathen beauty.'

I knew what words he was now awaiting from me. And I would soon be captured, not even having time to unsheathe my sword. I'd be put in shackles, cast into a dungeon. Was it a test? Yes! I saw how with a contrived casualness the master awaited a response from me. I stood with one side facing the door and saw the heavy curtains fluttering lightly in the wind, even though there wasn't the slightest breeze wandering in the room. I knew that beyond the curtains, ready to pounce, were the master's personal guards, the so-called panthers of the Rhine. Then I laughed and said:

'Not a very fortunate choice, master! Of course, if it has already been decided, I have no objections. I do say that it is unfortunate that the master did not discuss the matter with me before the taking of such an important decision.'

'You said that the general sense of the letter's contents were known to you,' the master replied, 'and I do not love to withdraw decisions that people in my charge have taken, especially as regards such a trivial matter as the fate of some unbaptised girl; it undermines the authority granted to me in the eyes of the people. Evian Steele knows better the local conditions. I do not want to interfere with his orders.'

'I agree,' I stated indifferently.

'That gladdens me. I had thought that you gave up your personal sympathies for the interests of the Order. My people had informed me that you were supposedly untrustworthy, which is why a small test for you was in order. I trust you. That will be my reply to the commander. My escort will accompany you. Go at once, fresh horses are awaiting you downstairs.'

'Master,' I said resentfully, 'my loyalty is unbreakable, unwavering, incombustible. Why was this deception with the immuring of the girl necessary?'

'It was not deception. The girl will be immured.'

Not uttering a word, I bowed and left.

My heart was beating unusually fast, I felt how the veins in my temples swelled; just one moment more and I would have given myself away. I was defeated, vanquished, wiped out. Evian Steele had a finer sense of smell, made more clever decisions, acted more cunningly. He had coordinated everything before laying his trap. Why had Steele read the letter, which was addressed to the master, out loud in front of me? At the time I did not wonder either at his strange openness, or at the fact that he didn't give me the letter personally to read. I thought he, that idiot, wanted to show off with his knowledge of reading and writing, the poor man, haughty as a turkey about it, because not all knights knew how to read and write. I had been cunningly misled. I was sent to the master so he could do what he wanted with Ulrika unimpeded. So, should I show my cards, dooming the revolt to failure, dooming the people to enslavement, or else sacrifice this victim? For the present I had not given myself away either with my words or my actions. I held fast, as a man should, however, as I got on my horse my foot slipped, and it was just with the help of the servant I was able to place myself in the saddle.

A shout of 'Ahoy!' rang out. With the planks of the bridge rattling under the horseshoes of the riders' regiment, we rode away from Riga Castle.

The Witching Hour

2

What would I do if I was a powerful dictator and would want to enslave a people, or what's more, if I wanted to wipe that people off the face of the earth?

I would come as a friend.

Open your heart and door to me, I will bring a palm branch in my right hand, and in my left hand I will bring a loaf of bread. I want to fill your barns and fulfil your longing, in order that peace and prosperity would rule over you.

If I would be rebuffed as a friend,

I would come as a brother.

We can choose our friends, but brothers come all on their own. Brothers appear with loud shrieks, and a mother's calm is turned into pain. All men are brothers, but I am not a brother because my mother's peace has not been turned into pain; my mother did not bear me, my father did not bear me, I have come into existence from nothing. I have been carried through the centuries in a veiny hand, and at four in the morning, while going to work, my father Mr. Dārziņš opened the entrance door of our building and stumbled on my cradle, on a wicker basket made from a bird cherry tree, where I lay small and sacred like a child of God. He stumbled and barely avoided smashing my fragile, tender child's head, but I lay calmly and quietly, a foundling without a name, without a homeland, without a past, brought through the centuries in the veiny palm of time. I lay like a fragile transparent sprout on the green branch of the tree of civilisation, and the roots of time stretched deep into civilisation's past, and civilisation was my homeland, my name, and Mr. Dārziņš lifted me up, took me inside, and Mrs. Dārziņš became my mother without pain, and without screaming.

Had I been born a Latvian, or a German, or Russian, or English, or Polish, or Czech, or Estonian, or Lithuanian, or a Swede? No one knows. But I got here straight from time's veiny palm, I grew together with the roots of this people, I laid down my roots deep. I reached the pain and serfdom, I got my own struggle, and in the branches many and varied leaves opened up to me.

The blue sky shone through the middle of a wide-open door. In the barn a horse was hanging by its legs from a beam; the head had already been cut off, the insides taken out. It was being skinned right at that moment. The butcher worked nimbly, cutting the lard with a sharp knife, tearing off the skin inch by inch from the still-warm trunk, while pounding it with a knife clenched in his fist to help the process along. His apron was spattered with blood, as were his trouser legs, arms and face. He shouted angrily at his dog:

'March right out of here!'

Out of here? Was I supposed to leave, or was that shouting for the dog? Maybe it was for me too? Why did I come here anyway, what did I want to find? Why did I, such a young man, have to get lost in the jungle of the past? I could go forward, I was going forward mightily, I am the best person in the world, the richest, the most socially insured, there were no ravines in the mountains of my future, I can be treated at a polyclinic for free (as an economist I know very well that I already paid for it earlier, as I was healthy, that both the healthy and the sick, everyone all the same, pays for being treated with taxes). I enjoyed a free education, as good as they could provide for me, I am honest, helpful, friendly, obliging, understanding, and I will live in communism. Why did I sneak into that old barn, where there was a horse hanging by its hind legs from a beam, with its head already cut off, its insides taken out, as the butcher was skinning it?

I am a tireless doer of work, a true twentieth-century hero, using my fame as an unconquerable revolutionary, an ardent champion of social transformation on the foundations of communism. I live in a resolute family of brothers, I together with my other brothers are united by a set of interests and goals, I am a tireless city worker, I carry the flag of socialist competition held high, I have a long-term goal – communism; I hold to the course of the victorious October, look, that's how I am, the statistical average. That's how I look at myself from the pages of magazines, from the columns of articles and reports, from photographs, from the TV screen. I am a superman. I am the best. I am the mightiest. Soon I will roar like a diesel engine, I will stomp the ground like an elephant, I will streak by like a supersonic fighter jet. Why do I need to clothe myself, eat, love? Why? I am so mighty. Let me be clothed, fed, loved! I, a person that's roaring, a person that can pat himself on the back, a person that's winning, a person going somewhere!

I have all possible freedoms: the freedom of gathering, the freedom of speech, the freedom of the press. I have all possible rights: the right to work, the right to holidays. I have everything, the only thing that falls to me is to produce, produce and once again produce; what falls to me is to become the very richest, the most cosmic, what falls to me is to simply produce, so that I can sit on five chairs instead of two, so I could eat three breaded pork chops instead of one, so I would have six suitcoats instead of two, so I would have twenty shirts instead of ten, so I would have six pairs of shoes instead of three, so I would have a separate room for the bathtub and a separate one for the toilet, so I would have my own flat, so I would have a refrigerator, so I would have a colour television, so I would have a savings bank book and electric heater, so I would have my own personal airplane.

I am a great cast-iron founder and the biggest caster of lies in the world. I have smelted millions and millions and millions of tonnes of steel, more than my ancestors in the Stone Age. I have milked more milk, laid more eggs, hatched more chicks. But am I passionate about it? Are those numbers beckoning me forward? What am I passionate for then? What then?

At times it seems to me that the world is one massive mistake, a massive question mark, an opened wound, a cry of pain, a misunderstanding, a scratch of black ink on the canvas of the Universe, and I can't sleep at night.

At least I can be open with myself, I can admit the fears to myself, the horrible fears, which torture me, and I am terrified of sleeping in the bosom of darkness and I look myself in the face with my eyes wide open. For now my thoughts are a secret, which I can discover, but I can also not discover them. For now, I say, for now, because no more than fifty years will pass and mind-reading machines will be invented, people will have their only prison taken from them, their only refuge – themselves.

I am a ball of contradictions, I am being unwound thread by thread, thread by thread on those dark nights of insomnia, nights when the earth is enveloped by darkness and people are enveloped by loneliness. At night the sky turns around the earth like a giant barrel with a silver spigot, in their own little world, fed through the spigot, more than a person doesn't know about the world around, black pitch rains down, the black pitch will take one away in the deep hole in the ice, lost in loneliness, white lightning appears over it, like a dog howling pitifully, at night, when the earth is enveloped by darkness and people are enveloped by loneliness, so why lock that loneliness in a ring? Why? Do the people really seize a sword, upon seeing an open heart? The people reach for their swords. Should one really put fear under lock and key in dungeons? Are the thinking really the renegades, and the doers the movers of life?

The Witching Hour

3

Before that I had entered the mind and body of Mr. Dārziņš.

It's no wonder some people harbour self-conscious illusions, though without really being conscious of it, that their life is an amazing occurrence, that they are something special, because, you see, they have been born, walk, eat, sleep, reproduce, and do everything else that people must do. The time comes, a person dies, and his offspring strides further along the same path, carrying in his heart a quiet belief, that his birth in and of itself has made life more meaningful, that with him being born he has accomplished his mission on earth with time to spare, and once again time passes, the end nears, and a person slides into non-existence, not suspecting that he was just a biological insect, an instrument, a massive machine of the state, a part of a lathe, stamping press or milling machine, a machine, which is not replaced with an actual machine only because in certain conditions live labourers are cheaper and the employer was unable to figure out where to put a freed-up worker. For him it means nothing, it's not the mind of an engineer, not the mind of a scientist, and no one asks why it isn't like that, because no one has to think, if everyone would start thinking, first of all the state would incur losses, because people would drink less spirits, and we all know that spirits are a mighty source of revenue, you could say one of the cornerstones of the budget.

It was in about this same style Mr. Dārziņš laid out his thoughts; he also remarked that the state's merciless mechanism grinds a person's personality into little bits and pieces and the only counterbalance lies in Cervantes's formula:

'Under my cloak I kill the king.'

I am an insignificant being in the state, however in me lies another, much more complete state; in it I am a subject and the head of the state, in it I make the laws and enforce them.

Mr. Dārziņš wore an ironed dark grey suitcoat. There could not be the slightest doubt that the shirt was white, brand-new, with a starched dickey, a tie with silver metallic thread, and a cane always at hand, the famous cane with the silver horse head. It was like a rule – to appear at work a half-hour early so he would manage to put on his switchman's uniform smelling of oil, steel dust and coal. At the end of his shift, Mr. Dārziņš also stayed in excess of half an hour, carefully washing himself and changing his clothes.

During the first days of the occupation, the railway was not in use; when Mr. Dārziņš once again needed to return to work, he took his luxurious suitcoat out of his closet.

'It will be too provocative,' Mrs. Dārziņš said. 'I am begging you, at least don't wear that English suitcoat, you know they're also fighting the English.'

'They're fighting practically the whole world, but why does a Latvian worker have to dress like a slob?' Mr. Dārziņš replied.

He returned home red from anger. Even his boss had supposedly praised him, saying:

'Well, well, very good, my man, we need to stand up and show that now, when we are once again free and Bolsheviks have been driven out, we can walk around like gentlemen.'

No one had noticed that Mr. Dārziņš's suitcoat was from English fabric, no one had spotted a protest to the occupational power in this demonstration, but quite the opposite – respect and approval. So the next time while getting ready for work, Mr. Dārziņš put on the worst rags, with boots going past the knee, an old raggedy sweater (which he usually wore when he heated the central heating in the cellar) and pants that had been sewn from what looked like a bag. It was an unbelievable sight, when Mr. Dārziņš went to the tram stop in the afternoon. The inhabitants of the neighbourhood, well-accustomed to his almost maniacal propensity to be well-groomed and well-dressed (which is why the switchmen also called him 'Mr.' Dārziņš) now gaped in astonishment. They said that it must be the finger of the occupiers, if that once respected craftsman (Mr. Dārziņš was also called the 'respected craftsman' because he knew how to do everything, for instance, replace glass in a broken window, put down hardwood flooring, whitewash the ceiling, carve chess pieces, and was happy to help people from work in his free time, taking a moderate fee for it), so, if a once respected craftsman like Mr. Dārziņš is walking around in a scarecrow's clothes, the finger of the occupation was apparently not clean.

In the second year of the occupation, Mr. Dārziņš came down with oesophageal cancer. After the operation he was taken home and fed with the help of a tube, food was relayed straight into his stomach. Difficult days began for Mrs. Dārziņš. Products were rationed, and Mrs. Dārziņš often went to the countryside to visit Rūlis, always returning with a full basket. In the winter of nineteen hundred and forty-three, while riding from the Rūlis family's home to the station, the horse veered off from the road, Mrs. Dārziņš fell off the sleigh, and they only found her the next morning – frozen to death.

Gradually I got used to the smell of raw flesh, the smell of rotting flesh, to something slimy and sticky, which floated through the air like a jellyfish, a transparent, elusive medusa jellyfish. The worse Mr. Dārziņš felt, the more this smell spread. It became so powerful that in the morning before coming into our room, Asters's wife Anna covered her mouth and nose with gauze soaked in vinegar. She poured medicine into the tube, then food, took out the bedpan, cleaned the room a little and left as quickly as was possible. Every sixth day she bathed Mr. Dārziņš. She was friendly and accommodating towards her patient. She invited me several times to sleep downstairs, in Asters's flat, on their small couch, however I refused, because, first and foremost – some officer from the commandant's office was quartered there, and secondly – I couldn't leave Mr. Dārziņš, because he didn't have any loved ones in the world anymore. It was true that Asters was considered his closest friend, but since the first days of the occupation some sort of transformation had occurred with Asters, and Mr. Dārziņš reminded him that if he wanted to kiss someone's behind, he needed to clean the spot with soap first, and then Asters did away with his old friendship, rented out the best room to an officer from the commandant's office and not once went upstairs to see the patient; but his wife, the good and warm-hearted soul Anna, didn't leave us in the clutches of fate. With Anna's help Grīzkalniete appeared. She began living in our flat, and then one day I found out from Grīzkalniete that I had been found in front of the door and Mr. Dārziņš, while going to work early in the morning, tripped over the basket, and the respected craftsman's black bowler hat rolled off his head, falling into a pot of dahlias near the steps.

The Witching Hour

4

After Mr. Dārziņš's death, the Asters family moved into our flat, beforehand airing everything out, but I was sent to the countryside to Rūlis. I became friends with Uncle Hans. He guarded the warehouse, but in his free time, as much free time as an army man can have, he helped Rūlis on the farm.

'A *gut* horse, a *gut* boy!'

Uncle Hans liked horses. He sat me on the back of a horse, he went along with me, stopping the horse with the reins, patting the steed on the back of his withers with his big hand. He was a wonderful friend, back in the *Vaterland* he had a farm, a wife, two *gut* boys and many *gut* horses. For him they were all dear – his *Vaterland*, his wife, his '*gut* boys' and '*gut* horse'. Such little Latvian boys differed little from the small German boys, the entire world's little boys are similar, but I was very similar to Uncle Hans's boys: I had blue eyes, flax-coloured hair, I was a completely '*gut* boy'; he could bounce me on his knee, throw me up in the air, he could sit me on the back of a horse. I liked all of that, and Uncle Hans seemed to be a great friend.

When the farmers from the area brought their young colts to Rūlis and the veterinarian came, Uncle Hans had a spare moment so he could help in castrating the colts. The day had heated up in the sun, and the dozen colts were fidgeting restlessly near the fence of the enclosure. Three more colts were brought in, and the operation could then begin. The colts were sweating, muscular and rowdy, their nostrils flaring, their eyes gleamed. They dug into the ground with their hooves, throwing their heads up high, whinnied towards the sun, and the entire paddock rang out, it smelled of pungent horse sweat. The first colt was taken close to the work bench, and the farmer held it down tight in the bridle. The colt went prancing, twisting sideways, chewing on the despised bit, with foam coming out of his mouth.

Uncle Hans quickly and nimbly slipped a noose over the colt's legs, and another three men came to hold it down, pushed their shoulders into the colt's sides, pulled the animal down to the ground, rolled it on its back, and tightened the rope around its legs near the ankles above the fetlocks (so it couldn't slide off). They held the colt down. They placed two smooth hewn beams under each side so the colt wouldn't try breaking free. One of them put a clamp on its lips and twisted it around so it would hurt less. Then the veterinarian could start his work, and Uncle Hans helped him, sometimes patting the colt on the inside of its hips and saying '*gut* horse,' sometimes throwing a glance in my direction and saying '*gut* boy.'

The colt snorted deeply, moaned, and its eyes bulged out as the pincers clicked, cutting through the spermatic cord. A moment later the operation was done, and the animal jumped up on its feet. It tried to run around but it was apparent that the poor horse was hurting.

The gelding once again bellowed, as it was taken past the shed where the mares stood, bellowed, not comprehending anything yet, not suspecting anything, once again fully fresh, sweating, muscular, but it was all over, its mission had come to an end, it was acknowledged as unsuitable for the continuation of the breed, destined for the brutal fate of a work horse; it was only granted the right to live one generation in this world. It once again bellowed, not suspecting anything, but the farmer's wife had taken its sperm gland to the kitchen in a brown clay bowl, because the veterinarian had told them to make a delicious meal – he was a gourmet, he knew what was good, what was bad, what was to be discarded, what you could fry, and at dinner the men sat at a common table in an enjoyable atmosphere, devouring the flavourful dinner, drinking juniper vodka along with it

I went into the shed, where the group of castrated colts stood with their tails tied; one of the farmers was on guard duty, looking to see that the geldings didn't lie down, otherwise the wound could get infected. Now they would be taking care of the geldings, feeding them with nice-smelling hay, they would care for them, pour crunchy oats into their trough, because a good farmer knew that for a horse to pull a wagon, it had to be fed well, it had to be allowed to rest and every once in a while had to be stroked.

I couldn't say I felt sorry for the colts, a boy rarely feels sorry for anything, the only thing I was tormented by was curiosity for what they would say when they found out what had been done to them.

The Witching Hour

5

Uncle Hans had gone to the front, he had already vanished from memory, when the war rolled west right over the Rūlis farm. The truth be told, there wasn't any battle in the area, the big and important roads were too far away, there was just a rare shot traded between small pockets of resistance and the aggressors. A few days later in the early evening some men decided to walk around the fields to see if the cows could be let out to pasture without worry, the small pasture ground that amounted to about two-thirds of a hectare near the house was full of holes and eaten up till it was bare, moreover it was still long to go before the frosts came.

They wanted to make me stay at home, but I ran to go along with the grown-ups. I was told to follow them closely, to not run off, not play around and not touch anything without the knowledge of a grown-up. Rūlis, his son Ernests and a neighbouring farmer led us. Clusters of alder trees and low-lying junipers bloomed in the pasture. Before retreating a small detachment of soldiers had been here, now the ground was littered with emptied tin cans, grey strips of newspapers, and spent cartridge shells. In the valley under the pines one could make out an abandoned outdoor kitchen, a pot on wheels. Having decided that it was safe for the cows to pasture there, the men walked further, and I followed closely behind. An occasional cluster of oaks began, with clumps of fern fans spread about. Before even getting to one of the oaks, the men stopped and I heard an order:

'Stay here.'

They went ahead, stopped, bent over a dark kill in the grass, and then I also, driven by an insatiable curiosity, snuck up to them.

In the tall grass, Uncle Hans was lying on his back, with his uniform unbuttoned. One of his legs, I didn't notice in the confusion whether it was the left or the right, one of the trouser legs had been cut through lengthwise and rolled up to his waist, and a yellowish bandage the colour of an old map was wrapped around his hip to the groin, as if it was covered with drops of seal wax. Hans's face was thin and yellow like a roll of wax with which the men waxed thread before mending the stirrups. There was a small blackened hole in his temples.

'He shot himself,' Rūlis said.

'He didn't want to be taken prisoner.'

'Is it that German?'

'Yep.'

'Uncle Hans!' I said, jumping into the conversation.

'Hold your tongue, boy!'

'He was probably left in the rear, came to look for the only known house and then didn't get any farther than the pasture.'

'God knowns how he got here, we certainly weren't expecting to see that.'

'He was the mighty horse castrator!'

'He was for sure.'

'He was coming here injured.'

'More likely he was carried here.'

'He was robbed, there's nothing on him.'

'No papers?'

'Nothing.'

I was ordered to run to the house for a shovel, and the wives, having heard that Uncle Hans was lying in the pasture shot, or having shot himself ('The same man who guarded the warehouse last summer?' 'Yes, the same guy!') also came to look.

But more than a year ago in the warm and sunny strawberry season we had walked in these same pastures. To be more precise, it was just Uncle Hans that had walked, I sat on his shoulders, my legs swinging on his chest, with my hands dug into his-brown hair. Uncle Hans was a mighty horse, clippity-clop, clippity-clop, he galloped through the pasture snorting, stamping his legs on the ground, raising his head up high, whinnying against the sun, neigh, neigh, bellowing, not yet suspecting his approaching death, knowing nothing yet, but his days were already numbered, neigh, neigh, he galloped with me on his shoulders, once again fully fresh, muscular, sweaty, and I made him stop at the bunches of strawberries, and we both feasted on the sweet berries.

Even now I still remember the bitter smell of the uniform's material, as he threw me up on his shoulder. In that same uniform they buried him in a dug grave, a soldier without a name, without honour, without an honour guard, some wide claw-like spruce branches serving as a coffin. On the second day I came to look at the grave, the sand had been evened out considerably by the rain in the night, the clumsily nailed cross knocked down by the wind or some animal – laying diagonally on the grave. Uncle Hans was my friend, which is why every summer, while taking the cows out to pasture, I remember to tidy his grave.

I stayed to live at the Rūlis farmhouse, and it was there I started to go to school as well, and in my free time, already as an adult, I helped with the farm work.

Rūlis would wake me up at six in the morning and we would go to the shed; already at the time a collective farm had been established and the animals were housed in the farm's buildings. I helped to feed and water the horses, to cart out the manure, put water from the well into a big barrel, while after breakfast we chopped firewood in the woodshed, as the January wind howled in the yard, throwing white whirlwinds of snow in the doorway.

In the afternoon I would help carry armfuls of hay and put them in the troughs; they were very small armfuls and Rūlis was the one who divided them up. The collective farm lived in poverty, we needed to save the hay, and it often happened that a horse, the first to get hay, would eat the entire trough before the last horse even got his first portion.

After lunch I read for a few hours, then it was once again back to the shed. While Rūlis cleaned out the manure, I chopped up sugar beets; while Rūlis gathered them up together with oats and poured them into the troughs, I pumped water from the well, and then around six thirty, when the work had been done and Rūlis, with a scraper in one hand and a horse comb in the other, stood in the stall next to a dirty animal so he could rub it clean, I saddled up Ancis, a fast brown horse, and with light but warm clothing on, went out into the blizzard.

Ancis knew the way well, there were places where we needed to manoeuvre carefully, there were places where we could go full speed. I was riding to get the mail. Rūlis was a big newspaper reader, as was normal for a farm, and he had subscriptions to all possible newspapers and magazines. The saddle made a crunching sound, and through the clothes my calves touched the breathing sides of the horse, the warmth of my body merged with the warmth of the horse's body.

On the main road, where the snow hadn't iced over, I bent over Ancis's neck and the horse went full speed, and I, lightly stroking him, patting the horse's neck, prodding and ratcheting up the speed of the sprint with an ever-constant 'go, go, go', got Ancis to reach a speed where the earth flew around like a record under the needle and the snow started whistling in my ears.

The Witching Hour

6

The wind was whistling in Ancis's ears as he galloped, he knew the way well, but there was a time when he didn't know anything, singing in the ears and running, clip-clop, clip-clop, time sang a blizzard song. It was also sung to Mrs. Dārziņš that awful night, that awful winter, when her husband was lying ill on his deathbed. It was Mrs. Dārziņš's last song, but Rūlis sat on the coach box and didn't see anything, he didn't know the way, no one knew the way, the driver was blind, the horse was blind, the earth was blind, the blizzard forced your eyes shut, the blizzard whistled in your ears, the blizzard stung your face, the blizzard stung your eyes, your eyes, your sharp eyes became narrow like arrow slits, one eyelid stuck to the other eyelid like embrasures around the barrel of a machine gun, clip-clop, clip-clop. Mrs. Dārziņš's legs were fat like those of an elephant mother in the zoo, and she herself was fat like the man-mountain in the film *The Gladiator*. She was a good target, heavy, immobile, which is why Rūlis sat on the coachbox, and not on the back seat, Rūlis was in the very front, with the wind in his throat, the wind howled a blizzard song, spewing snow clouds, snow clouds being spewed, clip-clop, clip-clop, a late-night train was going to Riga, to Ririririiigagaaa! And Mrs. Dārziņš fell from the sleigh, as a small bump in the road made it lurch sideways. Mrs. Dārziņš fell off, wrapped tightly in Rūlis's big fur coat, with a wide belt tight around it, two thick blankets around her ailing legs, and a basket of food near her feet, a helpless child, a cocoon, an immobile being, and Ancis, a young and rowdy horse, red like a fox, red like fire, its first winter in a harness, lost his way, it wasn't a surprise, the blizzard also sang in the horse's face, it wasn't a surprise, the blizzard sang in the eyes of the whole world, the bullets incessant like snow, the bullets burned like salt in the cheeks, the chest, stomach, joints, head, heart, the bullets burned like salt, much deadlier, much deadlier, a bee buzzed in the sweet pea blossoms, death sang the blizzard song in the throats of cannons, and blood trickled into the expanse, becoming stars, and that is why there are so many stars in the sky, but that night no one saw anything, their eyes were narrow as arrow slits, their gaze burned like the barrel of a machine gun. Run, Ancis, run, the red horse, run, fox, a flame, a fire snake, let it warm your sides like warm blood, run with the blizzard in your mane. It was just at the station Rūlis noticed he was alone, he searched the entire night, the horse went around in circles through the fields, lost, humanity was lost that night, and Mrs. Dārziņš froze; run, Ancis, the red horse, a fox, a flame, a fire snake, get lost, get lost in the fields, search for her, search for her!

After returning home late at night, I walked the horse into the shelter of the yard to cool it down. I put Ancis in the stall, I saw foam still trembling on his groin.

I returned to the city. Years went by. Once, when I went to visit the Rūlis family, by chance I walked through the horse pastures, looking for Ancis. I asked old Mrs. Rulis.

'Where's that horse I had?'

'You mean Ancis? They shot it, the poor thing,' the old woman replied. 'If you'd a come yesterday, you still would have seen it, but early this morning they shot it. It'll feed the pigs.'

'Who shot it?'

'Lediņš. He already got rid of all the old ones here.'

Spurred by a deep curiosity, I went to the shed a few kilometres away, and it really was so – the blue sky shone through the wide-open doors, and in the shed under the beams the horse was hanging from its hind legs, the head had already been cut off, the insides were spilling out, and they were just skinning it. The butcher worked quickly, with a sharp knife cutting off the fat, tearing the skin off inch by inch from the still warm trunk, using the knife handle held tight in his hand to help with the skinning. His apron was spattered with blood, as were his trouser legs, hands, and face. He yelled angrily at the dog:

'March right out of here!'

They threw a black bag over Ancis's head, so he could stand calmly, so he wouldn't be afraid. They raised the barrel up and put it to his ear, there, where the softest fluff billows around the cartilage like smoke, where the ear, like pastry strands that have been twisted together, is growing from the head, it was there they put a cold barrel smelling of powder. Clippity-clop, clippity-clop! It's strange, but it seems to me Uncle Hans died almost the same way; most likely several of the soldiers retreated together, Uncle Hans was wounded, heavy, they couldn't carry him any longer, so in the night, as he slept, they covered his face with a handkerchief, a barrel against his temple, and it was over. Clip-clop, clip-clop! Uncle Hans was my friend. And all people are brothers. It's just they don't know it.

Open your heart and door to me, in my right hand I will carry a palm branch, and in the left I will carry a loaf of bread. I want to fill your barn and fulfil your longings, so that peace and prosperity would rule over you.

If I am rejected as a brother,

I will come as a friend.

If I was a mighty dictator and would want to enslave a people, or even more, if I wanted to wipe that people off the face of the earth.

The Witching Hour

7

The occupation punished the people, punished them physically, biting and sucking out the juices of life. For the conquerors, the rank and file man was just a biological insect, which needed to be taken advantage of as quickly as possible and then eliminated using the least painful methods possible, and that is what was done. Mr. and Mrs. Dārziņš were destroyed by the occupation, hardly finding out about their existence, without so much as laying a finger on them. The very fact of the occupation turned out to be sufficiently deadly. It was otherwise with Asters.

A clerk at the Ministry of Education, physically strong, with a tenacious will to live and a relatively high mental capacity, but not so high as to be able to think independently, Asters was above all pliable, useable. Asters proved to be a prostitute, and the many-headed hydra of the occupation deepened Asters's prostitution even more, dredged it like a ditch, like a drainage canal, and Asters flowed ahead, gushing, swirling the dirty waters. While putting together study programmes, he was friendly and gave his all to everyone, like he gave his all to Kārlis Ulmanis, like he gave his all to Adolf Hitler, and, if a miracle would happen, and the earth was conquered by Martians, he would also give his all to them just as heartily. All of his thoughts, his opinions he subordinated to orders down to the letter; he made himself subordinate to the 'New Knowledge', he subordinated himself to his 'Fatherland' in the strictest way, and, if some Martian newspaper would write that on earth children grow in flower pots, he would also subordinate himself to that. Being wide and voluminous, Asters took in everything, from everyone and everywhere. If a person sold his body, maybe that's a necessity, but if he sells his soul? These kinds of spiritual prostitutes were cultivated during all the years of the occupation, because a regime can only exist when there are people within a nation that endlessly betray the nation.

'If it wasn't for us,' they say, 'then the nation would be slaughtered, exterminated, wiped off the face of the earth, scattered all about, we are doing holy work, we are saving you from total annihilation, sacrificing ourselves on the altar of the fatherland. You think we have it easy? We chose a lesser evil from all possible evils after all, and it's unimaginable that you want to be free from all obligations, you understand after all that there's a large army near Moscow or not far from Moscow, a large army is near the walls of Leningrad or close to its walls, there is one near the Volga or close to it, soon, very soon the land up to the Urals will be ours, yes, yes, you heard right, it will be ours as well, because the mighty Grossupertramtramland will take us in its charge, under its warm, motherly wings so it can protect us from the pillaging, so it can protect us from the world's plutocracy, thanks to the mighty Grossupertramtramland, thank you! Thank you, that its tanks are in our cities, that its soldiers dance with our girls at parties, thank you! We aren't respectable enough for us to continue our kind. The Führer wants, the Party wants, that all nations, that we together with all nations, that they would flow into a united, mighty Europe, that this is so powerful, finally fulfilling the ancient dream of man about unity in one whole, triumphant, fertile, all-encompassing organism, discarding the old prejudices out like old shells, hip hip hurray!'

Earlier for the conqueror masses it was hard to get around, it was just the lords and soldiers that made their home here, so where would a simple colonist get enough resources from in order to ship his personal belongings thousands of kilometres away?

In the twentieth century, iron horses with endless rows of wheels would be at the disposal of each that so desired. As soon as war would end with victory, colonists would appear. The administration would rule with a heavy hand, it would invite those wanting land there, those coveting an easy life, those searching for happiness, a select few, the shopkeepers of souls, and they would roll in an unending string there from their own overpopulation (the Fuhrer wrested living space!), they would rain down, fall, tumble like hard hail from the sky, together with '*gut* wives, *gut* boys, *gut* girls, *gut* Nazism', and in a flash – we would become a wonderful colony, a wonderful slaughtering ground, because what the Order didn't do in seven hundred years, the Führer would accomplish, hip hip hurray!

'What is eating you up so much about the occupation? Weren't we friends? Did I have something like that on my mind? It all ended such a long time ago, you're walking on the face of the earth healthy and whole, the future belongs to you, but I am lying in a forest near the Rūlis family, and my loved ones don't even know where my grave is!'

Oh! Uncle Hans. There's a damp metallic sound in my voice, my friend has been lying in his grave for twenty years already, pine needles and small maggots were in my voice, dust was in my voice, and the strangest thing was that during those twenty years Uncle Hans, while lying in his grave, had learned Latvian. I would bet that if he would be walking on the face of the earth, he also wouldn't know more than '*gut* boy' and '*gut* horse'.

The Rooster Hour

1

Shoobie doobie,

a button nose, a little eye, my little bunny, a velvety cheek, a celestial mask, a cute little face.

Shoobie doo wop–wop.

The girls' thin legs flash by in dance, those who can't find home roam the night, what a sight, night, everyone goes the whole night through, a shallow grave in soft sand is dug,

and so on and so forth, most likely some wires got crossed in my brain. Fried from long hours of work. I didn't take a holiday last year.

A senseless life of sensational nonsense that people sense is pointless.

But all in all I am still strong and hope to live to sssseventy-ffffour.

Seventy-four? Not bad. I am the oldest person in the world, if you look at the statistical data. Soon they will all be envious of me, maybe also hate me. People who are doing better, are always hated by those who are doing worse. Regardless of whether it's physically, or spiritually, it doesn't matter. Gastronomically. In this day and age we are famous for eating. The great gluttons, in other words. We would gladly trade everything for good food, and thus we consume and devour our trips, our cars, our family homes. In that sense there are no limits whatsoever. It's been declared that other things, for example freedom, you can't eat, otherwise we'd start on that too. For the time being we are hocking a thing or two at the pawnshop, so we can eat our fill.

In the pawnshop, Continental typewriters rattle without abate, piles of pawn tickets, and it's like that every day, every day there was a serpentine queue, strange people, who don't know how to plan a family budget, it's impossible for any other troubles to exist in our social incubator, and those who don't understand how to plan swim in the smell of naphthalene, they never had enough money, so they would pawn their last clothes, their last silver spoons, gold snuff boxes, bracelets, watches, rings, whoever has gold, those filthy rich people, they don't have to stand in queue, in that massively long queue

you smell of caraway seeds, you are my dear caraway seed bunny

together with the ragged, there's a shorter queue near the gold things, the silver things, it's an almost or entirely humane queue, it's not serpentine.

The payment was made in another room, and about twenty people huddled around the cashier's window. A middle-aged man fidgeted like he was on hot coals, he had to go to a wedding, his relatives were getting married, you see, and he didn't have money for a wedding gift, so he got a loan, but that lowlife money lender asked for it back three hours later, having lost all sense of shame and decency; he had heard some rumours, he had heard through the grapevine from some woman, he had taken her word for it, so he was asking for the money back, the gift was already bought, the money was used up, he had to bring the watch and both rings to the pawnshop, he never should have gotten that loan, it would have been better to steal than borrow money, at least not a new ring, not the rings for the wedding. He had to go. To the sauna. He had to shave. His beard. (He craned his head out over the crowd.) He was a witness. He just couldn't. Head to the altar without taking a bath, unshaven, sorry, not to the altar, they were getting married in a civil registry office, he had misspoken, damn it, on top of it he had to stand in the queue to get his own money, were they finally going to open? (No one listened to him, he was muttering to himself, for his own enjoyment.)

She sells sea shells by the sea shore, the shells she sells are surely seashells, so if she sells shells on the seashore, I'm sure she sells seashore shells.

The cashier's window opened, and the poor masses, the money-hungry mob of people with empty pockets, threw themselves at the window. Their arms stretched over one another. Their nervous fingers, manicured, painted, dirty, bitten, long, pretty nails pawed for the pawn tickets. The penholders were worn-out, the dip pens were done for. The ink was violet. I needed to sign. That I am happy with the appraisal. The date. Me. Then once again stand in line at the cashier's window to take it. The money crinkles pleasantly. Like the lingerie of a beloved woman, the mutterer says, then leaves and disappears. Das Kapital. Old Marx. Students stretching their stipends for their stomach, striding along in a sanctioned society. Those who have money don't think about it. When we don't have money, we go, go to the street, go to friends' places, go to the pawnshop, go somewhere. Money provides weight, edible weight, drinkable weight, enjoyable weight, transportable weight. As a student, every spring I would pawn off my winter coat. Until I had worn it so much that they wouldn't take it anymore.

A tiny dormouse. A little cutie pie.

The king of the fleas.

The Rooster Hour

2

The girls vibrated in dance, the skirts twirling around their waists in colourful wheels, their slender legs flashing in white socks, clickity-clack, a touch, leather heels, wrought shoe buckles, clinkity-clink, a jump, a firm grip, flying, girl, flying, flying, throw her up, once again, once again, throw her up, flying, flying, girl, flying, holding close, a jump, clinkity-clink, shoes with wrought buckles, leather heels, a touch, clickity-clink, slender in white socks flashing, skirts spinning in colourful wheels around their waists, girls twirled in dance, a slice, a slice of bread, spread, thread, shred, tread, the parents need to think long and hard when they choose a name for their children. Ulrika. They also made fun of me. I'd like to see Eddy one but you. They couldn't come up with anything else, in school, that was a long time ago.

I am waiting on the street, and soon the dancers emerge from the concert hall in a merry gang. Ulrika's cheeks are as rosy pink as carnations, she recognises me, we walk together for one block, and I am already accepted into the group, acknowledged as one of their own. Where are we going now? Oh, one of the nice girls here apparently has a summer cottage close to Riga, we will go there.

The train is packed. Everyone hurries to get out of the city. Brown beer bottle corks pop, beer foam runs out, it rains into dry throats, and then you hear midsummer celebration songs. In the garden near the summer cottage, there in the rose garden near Sans-souci, we were stealing kisses there.

The bonfire in the dark of night glowed, have mercy on me, my love, have mercy. I pressed Ulrika up against a tree, it was a linden, I kissed Ulrika greedily, I was going to squeeze her into the tree, her back was against the linden, her stomach touched my stomach, I hid my hand behind the neckline of her blouse, I kissed her like crazy, my movements were shameless, I myself became the tree. You can't do that, don't do that!

Yes, yes, yes!

The intoxication vanished. My head was cool and clear like a deep well. Blood was pulsating everywhere.

Not here, we can't do it here.

Let's go, let's go.

We left into the darkness, in a tight embrace, until it hurt, two people, our limbs blazed like logs in a fire, until it hurt, good we left into the darkness, we left the clamour, the noise, we left the rounds of beer bottles, we left society, we left the words, we left the songs, we left the music, we left to visit the snake in the Garden of Eden, we left to go into ourselves.

Ulrika's hair flew around her head like molten gold in the sunrays, it smelled of lavender and rosemary oil, thick, light, the yellow morning sunrays slid into the train wagon's window, green fields, the forests slid by, people, houses, roads, a car slid by, changing, we slide back to the city, the night passes by behind our backs, Ulrika is sleeping, her head resting on my shoulder, her eyelashes had nothing applied to them, and later I find out that she's never used makeup in her life, only on stage, and so she is sleeping, her hair flying about around her head like molten gold, it smells of lavender and rosemary oil, thick, light yellow morning sunrays slide into the train wagon's window, green fields, the forests slide by, the colourful little people, little houses from toy blocks, snake roads, beetle cars slide, change, and suddenly a tear slides down from Ulrika's eye, and the tear slides downwards on Ulrika's cheek, and Ulrika awakens, and said 'I dreamt that you had left me.'

The Rooster Hour

3

The unknown woman stirred on my couch, stretched a round white arm from under the blanket, turned on her right side and went on sleeping. I didn't know anything about her yet.

The Rooster Hour

4

But I was protecting myself against falling in love. That is why I am happy. Peace. To not become attached to anyone or anything. But this wasn't funny anymore. Her hair was thick, light yellow, flying about her head like molten gold in the sunrays, the scent crawled into my soul like the sweet honey of forest bees, I could fall in here, become trapped like a bear with a sweet tooth in a noose, I could be forced to make children, be yoked to a family, all of those things, chicken, cluck, cluck, chicks, cheep, cheep, little ones, come here, dears, I was threatened with a strange and unknown life, no, no thanks, give it to the next guy.

Ulrika was lovable, desirable, conquerable, enjoyable, but at the same time also something that was totally foreign, unknown, frightening. Until now I had avoided women who cry in their dreams. Far too serious in our devil-may-care age. Easily, lightly, fleeting. Well, if they toss their legs about (the girls' slender legs flashing in dance), then their character isn't one of the more difficult ones. What a downer. Of course, during the first few months I didn't feel apprehension, fear, worry. I swam in love like honey. And suddenly I was in a cauldron. And I was being boiled. And it was hot. This was no laughing matter. Everything matched, the characters, the thoughts, everything fit, was smoothed over, got stuck together all the more, more and more inseparable.

I didn't want to become tied-up, stuck together, fit. To live means to enjoy? Why the hell not! I worked. I was not a bad employee. I worked well. I would hide in my work. I know how to generalise, analyse, draw conclusions. Sacred qualities. If you make something, then make it well. Everything else is secondary. Work is the only thing. Long live numbers and number people. In this quarter raising the capacity by eight and a half percent and three-fourths of a percent, we will achieve it, we will attain, we will surpass last year's results by so many and so many tonnes. And the kitchen, comrades, don't forget it, a good cook at the fore of a good and honest team of cooks in reality leads the factory. Don't give them food with too much pepper, it will make the workers nervous, don't give food that is too bland, it will make the workers idle. Compared with last year, electric power, leather shoes, coal, crude oil, steel, cement, cotton fabric, silk fabric, and sugar production have grown. Refined sugar is made from our homeland's raw materials. Three hundred and seventy-three kilos of steel (per each inhabitant's soul). This and that person fulfilled the plan for next year and the year after and is working on the year after that. One automobile wheel rolled away two kilometres ahead of the others (meaning the remaining three). What should we do, make the other three go faster or stop that one upstart? At least one thing was clear, there was something wrong with the car.

AND ME?

I must work. I must work. No question. So then I gave it my all. I don't steal time from work one bit. Always like a nail, like a bayonet. I dump my brains on the table, roll up my sleeves to my elbows, rummaging around the greenish mush, looking for a suitable idea, a new insight, an untapped reserve. That is my task. To dig around deep in my brain mush. Most likely some wires had gotten crossed in my brain. I'll be burnt out because of the long hours. I didn't take a holiday last year, I had a sudden business trip, and also Ulrika, my honeybun, my sweetiepie, began to scare me with her love. Her love buried me like an avalanche. I had never been buried like that before. Under an avalanche. Forgive me, mountain climbers. But I feel it. I felt it.

The order is simple – school, studies, work, family, death. A citizen's path and duties. A vicious circle, and then start everything over again from the beginning? A person realises that they are not eternal, and takes steps in advance to care for the continuation of his stock on earth, he finds allies for himself, he continues himself with life, not with work, work is as indispensable as air, indispensable as sleep, however a secondary matter, the first is and remains a living being in the eternally lush throng of humanity, while work – it is just fruit, bunches of it each autumn, and work revolves around a person, like the planets revolve around the sun, and not the other way around. However, I still didn't believe it, I was raised like a bent tree, just under one wind, work, work, we all revolved around work, and the rest I let slip out of my hands, the rest I enjoyed, I didn't believe that I would be trapped in the next stage as well, I fought against it, I struggled even though my voice as well rang out in the iron barrel of life like the squeak of a little mouse, like the buzz of a mosquito, like a small pipe in the powerful roar of an organ's bass notes; the state had received my work, but would they then also take the flesh of my flesh? Could the honey-licking bear become the beekeeper smoking out the bees?

I ran away to my business trip, but it wasn't a long separation at all, because Ulrika arranged some days off for herself and one day, just half a week had passed, and one day I saw Ulrika's hair in the hotel lobby. She had scraped together some money, arranged some days off for herself, and overcame a thousand small obstacles, and flew in, just to be with me. She couldn't live even three days without me.

Three days, the first three days were the hardest ones.

It's easy for you to say, you're strong.

And then the next ones are easier.

You're also cruel.

Yes. The first three scratched like a cat's claws.

Well, please, don't be angry.

I spoke with the hotel director so he could arrange a separate room for us, he informed us that there supposedly wasn't a room available and we shouldn't be allowed to live in one room together as an unmarried couple; a moralist, maybe he had a daughter Ulrika's age, but after a long and tiring haggling a room ultimately appeared.

A good room. A shower. A bathtub. Hot water at any time. During the day, at night, in the morning, in the evening. In the tub. In the shower.

The Rooster Hour

5

There were two cherry-red couches in the room, each wide enough that we could both lay down together on them. The hallway was separated by double doors and entrance area, no one could surprise us here, no one could hear us here, it was a true Garden of Eden, but what was lacking here was an angry Lord, who would drive us out after our fall into sin, and it wasn't a sin here, we murdered one another, we strangled one another, we gnawed at one another, we ate, licking the chewed-up bones with pleasure, and the couch was impassioned together with us, and we fell for a moment in the tub, splash, and we walked around naked, wet legs on the bathroom floor, and dried each other with towels, and once again returned to the room, and began everything from the beginning. We couldn't allow ourselves anything like that at home, neither at Ulrika's parents' place on those rare occasions when we stayed for the night, they both had ears as sharp as a ground squirrel, a mouse, a rabbit, the sharp and destructive ears of a moralist, we also couldn't behave so uncontrollably at my place; if a spool of thread fell in my room, then the good, kind-hearted soul, Asters's wife Anna, would get on her knees in their room to look for it, which is how the walls so fully and clearly did away with secrets. It didn't bother me, let them listen and think what they want, however in such cases Ulrika was unsurpassably self-conscious, the thin walls ruined all the fun for her. I understood that, it's not hard to understand that at all, you just need to imagine for a moment that you are the other person, imagine it for a moment, really imagine it in detail, and all the joy

73

was ruined for us at home. Although the radio also always blared full blast. However, you weren't allowed to turn it on at night, the whole house would wake up.

So, the best week ever went by in that hotel room. The best week ever? The best automobile in the world. The first car was built by a guy named Daimler in eighteen hundred eighty-six. It was the best automobile in the world. Then others built their own best automobiles in the world. Fords, Pontiacs, Cadillacs, Buicks, Oldsmobiles, Fiats, Chevrolets, Citroens, Dodges, Mercedes-Benzes, Lincolns, Volgas, Moskviches, Chaikas, and every other car was the best in the world at some point. There was one automobile after another, and each following car was better. One week passed and another came, and here the regularity lost its pull. The only good week. And that's all? Where were the others, where was technological advancement, where was the development of productive capacities, where were the new planning methodologies? Plan me one more good week! Dear economist, Comrade Dārziņš Eduards, Eddy! You say you can't? Plan me one! Where are your reserves after all, why don't the subordination systems work, or did the raw material production stop? No, raw materials are being produced just as uninterruptedly and timely as before, I don't even know why I don't put my all into that issue and plan it. Just one week. It was, and will remain, the best. And won't there be better weeks in my life? Why are you doing everything to break free of Ulrika? Because I don't want routine, because I don't believe that there won't be a better week, because I want an airplane.

The Rooster Hour

6

The unknown woman on my couch turns on her other side, pulls the blanket up to her chin, and hides her naked white arm. Sleep. Slumber, serenity, supine, sinews. Symmetry. Smooth. Sharp. Sure.

The Rooster Hour

7

After a three-day journey we arrived at the borders of the commandry and on the evening of the fourth day, galloping at full speed, we saw the sun's golden shield disappear sideways behind the grey castle towers.

About five hundred paces from the fortification's walls loomed the partially destroyed walls of the unfinished temple of worship. It was clear that the vandals had once again worked hard at night and no one had disturbed them.

The commander was awaiting me, as was his broad, innocent-looking face (it did not fit his character, his fox-like cunning), and his face, his innocent-looking face beamed with joy about my early and happy return. For some unknown reason he took me under my elbow, as we walked through the giant outer bailey. His retinue, their spurs clinking, and armour clanging, followed us.

In the grand hall I gave him the master's letter. We had not uttered a word to one another until now. Evian Steele took off a glove, tucked it in his belt, and with his naked hand (in great respect to the master's parchment) unrolled the scroll. His retinue stood a respectable distance. Etiquette was strictly observed.

For four days on that long journey I had thought of a plan of action down to the last detail, everything was clear like the patterns of sword movements in a fencing hall. While reading the letter, the commander looked at me occasionally. I tightened my lips into a smile and said, hissing through my teeth:

'Where is Ulrika?'

The commander seemed startled by this unexpected sound, a broad smile appeared on his face (about my uncontrollable behaviour), and Evian Steele quietly and politely replied:

'The pagan girl has been imprisoned in the castle's small hall for guests.'

'You scoundrel,' I hissed, 'why were you playing the fool?'

No one heard us, as the conversation proceeded so quietly. Discourtesies expressed within a group of two is not an offence, which is why the commander replied:

'I delight in fooling the cunning.'

'You knew who she is to me, did you not?'

'How was I to know that? Why did you not bring her to the castle before? Why did she remain unbaptised? Now she will be walled in. She is the most beautiful pagan girl in the commandry, I cannot help you any more, besides, the master has written that you had supposedly agreed to it.'

'Yes. However, if a hair has been harmed on her head…'

'Had I imprisoned her in the cellar, it is not just the hair on her head that would have been harmed, you know yourself the kind of rats one can find there.'

'Do not think that we will escape unharmed!' I hissed.

A merry curiosity lit up the commander's face. Such an action surprised him. I knew he was ready to expect any ruse, however this behaviour almost knocked him from his saddle. We? Evian Steele and Bailiff Dārziņš? 'You will not escape alive,' that is what Evian Steele expected from me, and now he had to think that the bailiff, poor soul, was confused, and once again asked:

'What did you want to say with that?'

'You will see for yourself,' I replied.

Leaving the commander, I bid my farewell to the knights and brothers, and went to see Ulrika. Already in the corridor I understood that a private meeting would be almost impossible. The most trusted men of Evian Steele were on guard, and they were not able to be persuaded with cunning or bought off by gold, they only acknowledged orders.

'Let me through,' I said.

'There are orders not to let anyone through.'

'Do you know who I am?'

'Bailiff Dārziņš. But we cannot violate the commander's orders.'

'The commander cannot order me. It is only the master that is above me.'

'We hear you! But the commander gives us orders, we only fulfill his orders. It was ordered to not let anyone through.'

The guard's men openly ridiculed me. What else could be expected. It would be naïve to try and say anything more, only force helped here. I pushed the halberds of the guards up, but they had expected an attack and pushed me back without effort.

'Is the Holy Father also denied entrance here?'

'The Holy Father is allowed in.'

Even a clergyman had greater authority in my land. I once again bitterly felt that on the outside the honourable position of bailiff was in reality just the carnival mask of a joker.

'All glory be to Jesus Christ,' I said, entering the cell of the Holy Father.

'Forever and ever,' the old voice replied.

'Does the Holy Father know which girl Commander Evian Steele has chosen for his horrible task?'

'Yes, my son, I understand your consternation. Did you have a connection with the girl?'

'Ulrika is my bride-to-be.'

'Yes, my brother, but she does not want to become baptised, her fate will be an example to all other obstinate people, and the church's walls will not fall any longer, Satan's passions will be restrained. You blame the commander in vain, it is the very will of the master!'

'The master?'

'Yes, my son. I see that your heart is heavy. The commander warned me about you, but he is wrong about you, I am sure of it, I have always seen you close to God and the faith. I do not believe that the beautiful pagan girl has bewitched you, that you would throw away honour, fame, the future and power, for her.'

'Did the Holy Father attempt to turn Ulrika towards the true faith?'

'It was all for naught, my son, it would be easier to squeeze a tear from a stone than remorse from that stubborn girl.'

'I want to see her, Holy Father.'

'You are fighting in vain, my son. Of course, I would be able to arrange this. But you are sensible, my son, and with an imprudent step or word your future could be ruined. I am not allowed to reveal to you, but perhaps I could keep you from erring by revealing it. So listen. The Order would like to appoint you to a high post in the Baltic, and this is your test.'

'I already heard that from the master himself,' I replied. 'I feel honoured for the unexpected trust and I give up my intent to see Ulrika, however I cannot stay silent. Do you know what horrors through this ill-advised test the Order, the commandry, the fate of the state has been forced into?'

'Speak, my son.'

'The news about the immuration has already spilled over the borders of the land. We have finally given a pretext to the discontents to assemble into battalions and stand against the Order with fire and sword. It has become known to me that great forces are coming to the commandry's castle and that they will arrive no later than in four days.'

'What treachery,' the Holy Father said. 'Everything should have happened in the utmost secrecy. However, it has been expected and is even desired. Additional forces have been called in, we will drive out the rebellious spirit of the Latvians for all time.'

But I, my teeth nearly chattering out of fear, began to tell him how unprecedented the massive battalion of rebels was, the head-chopping, gut-ripping, and bone-breaking rebels were coming to the castle, that the castle was poorly defended, additional forces meant absolutely nothing, that it would be good to raise the wall a few feet, then the Holy Father objected, saying that:

'It does not matter, the mortar will not have enough time to set.'

However my arrows had hit their target, I saw that the holy father was deeply grateful for the insight of the situation and listened carefully, considering a few possibilities for defence in his mind, and less than half an hour later I was very sure that he would raise his ideas to the commander.

'What do you think, my son; are they capable of occupying the castle?'

'If we don't have enough stones to strike our attackers, then the castle will be occupied,' I exclaimed.

'Stones?' the Holy Father murmured. 'Stones? When did you say they would be here?'

'In less than four days.'

'Everything is going as was expected,' the Holy Father said. 'Then a messenger must be sent to the master and tomorrow the farmers must be ordered to bring at least twenty wagons of stones good for throwing.'

Deftly throwing back the lapels of his long mantle, the clergyman hurried from his cell. I could be content for the time being. The self-centered clergyman considered himself to be a great expert in war matters, of course, he would offer a freshly made idea from a hot pan to the commander – to bring at least twenty wagons of stones good for throwing. Well, yes, that is quite right!

Part Two

Monologues at Night

Dina's Monologue

This guy also said, you can't do that at home, well, I understood that, but also, I asked as a joke – why can't you? He replied, there was a mad dog in the house, I laughed, that's what they all called their wives, I asked, well is she really so mad? No, he really does have a dog, a hound, a pedigree beast, but he is crazy for bitches, and when the bitches are in heat, you can't keep him at home, maybe they need to neuter him. I said that you can neuter stray cats, but, well, I had never heard that you do it to dogs. Then we got into a taxi and he said a place so we could go somewhere. I thought that he could give some roubles to the driver right there in the taxi, the driver seemed like a good guy, so he could go and walk around for half an hour, and we had to leave the car clean, however he didn't even hint to the possibility of doing it in the car; it seemed he had some other place in mind. We drove almost to the lake, got out, he paid for the journey, I saw that he had money in his wallet. We went past the ship station, it was already dark, a strong wind was blowing, the lake splashed our legs, I was afraid to get my shoes wet and also was a little afraid of him, however he seemed so respectable and good-hearted, a real gentleman, and I went with him, and he was a little drunk, he told me he hadn't organised those sorts of gatherings, but he didn't say what kind of gatherings they were, fell silent and then began to whistle, he apparently loved lyrical songs, sweet, melodious ones, and me, what did I love? I said that I like jazz, the twist, he made a wry face, I supposedly had Western tastes, but well what could you expect, had I been working as one for a long time? I asked, how did he know what I did, that I am a proper girl. But he said that he had a trained eye, he could tell right away what kind of girl I was, he even knew how much I supposedly took for a night, he knew life just as well as I did, and then I asked what he did. But he just whistled and looked sideways, the whites of his eyes shone in the darkness, I got a bit scared, but what can you do, such is the job. I went with him to a little shed on the ship dock, the door was of course locked, but he picked it open lickety-split, I was thinking that I had gotten mixed up with a criminal, I had to admit that I was getting curious and I thought, it won't turn out well, and from the beginning he did what they all normally do. The door was blocked from the inside by a wooden plank, I took a good look at all of that while he lit up, striking two matches in the process. Then he started to grope me, babble on incoherently and force himself on me, he did what they normally do, and then he wanted to put out the cigarette, and by then I was already thinking that I won't be able to bear it, he did it with the cigarette between his lips, and the cigarette butt almost burned one of my eyes, and then he said he was going to put it out, and I started to scream, he put his hand on my mouth, that old devil, and wanted to do it forcibly.

For-ci-bly.

A crazy situation.

I was lucky, I kicked him in a delicate place, he was already quite old, well past sixty, he wasn't able to bear it, fell down, and while he scrambled to get up, I threw the door open and ran out, I ran, I had left my bag there, I couldn't even look back, he most probably was running after me, I knew I had to lose him, I wanted to run through a yard, hide on another street, but all the houses were with gardens, all their gates were locked, with barbed wire on top, I was already thinking that my end is coming, he will appear and it will be over for me, but then someone from the window, my only salvation in a time of need, because I was already weak, I was able to get to the window to see, I didn't see the old man, he most likely rummaged through my bag, it doesn't matter, there wasn't any money there, there wasn't anything there, so,

Monologue of Lonely Mother Frosya

She was once again drunk as a skunk, squealing loudly from quite a ways away,

'Frosya, Frosya!'

What are you yelling for, what are you yelling for, you dirty whore, it's two in the morning, the entire house is asleep, but she, that wasted wino, comes and howls like an animal under the knife, well, just that this boozer is plastered, what else does she do, and tonight I hear her again, she's running, running from the lake lost, roaming around the yard, dragging empty bottles from the rubbish bins with her, well, I thought, misfortunate is once again upon us, drunk, she's running, soon she'll shout out,

'Frosya, Frosya!'

She climbs over the fence, that obnoxious fossil, she doesn't try to go through the gates, so she climbed over the fence, and pounded, and drummed the window, holding onto the windowsill with one hand, that lowlife, no fear, no respect, she can't stay on her feet, I will let her in, we already know, we know, she'll sleep it off, wolf down everything in the building that's edible, and will waddle off to beg for a drink, the last time she took all the empty milk bottles, I brought milk for the little Grišiņš boy, and the little one also woke up, but he was understanding, the little sweetheart, the little treasure, not a sound, not a word on his lips, that old witch, I already explained to him yesterday to not listen to her by any means, if we don't answer her, she can't do anything to us, except,

'Frosya, Frosya!'

And then she lets go of the windowsill, pounds the window with both hands, oh, you, my misfortune, what will the people here think of me, will she be able to stand on her feet, boom, on the ground, crawling on all fours through the garden and crying, she's snorting in such a way that you can hear it for kilometres, and screaming,

'Frosya, Frosya!'

She's getting on my nerves, you could go crazy listening to it, and then someone couldn't bear it, they open the window, stick their head out, I hear from his voice that it's Asters.

'Frosya doesn't live here anymore, go away!'

Well, she starts to howl again, having heard the man's voice,

'Someone let me in, take pity on me, take pity on me!'

Who would take pity on her, that drunk whore, no fear, no respect, thanks to Asters, he understood that she's not my friend, that I'm not ready for misfortune, but can you really step into another person's shoes, but she just howls,

'I can't bear it, let me in, let me in!'

Now the entire house is up for sure, everyone hears her, they are listening, what will they think, Asters tells her,

'If you scream one more time and disturb our sleep, I'll call the militia, their car will be here in five minutes flat!'

He saved me, he doesn't have a telephone or anything, but it helps, oh, does it help, she settles down, calms down, abates, she climbs over the fence again, tears her skirt, I hear how it tears, she stumbles down the street, maybe a tram is still running, whisk her away to the city, what horror, can you really slip into another person's skin, all sorts of people are in the hospital, I, cleaning the floor, taking out the dishes, began to chat, I talked with everyone, it's easier for a person that way, if you throw a nice word their way, she was quite nice, her face was the worse for wear, she came to visit me, a bottle in her pocket, hey, let's drink, well, I didn't get out of that so easily, Grišiņš, the little guy, little sweetie pie, clever little boy, so cleeeever, he didn't say a word, it would be nice if Valerijs came now, oh he could come now, he would say in a low voice, make yourself scarce and don't ever come here again, decent people live here, but what was that to him, I didn't utter a word about a wedding or something like that, but he felt, the bastard, he felt that I could tangle him up, he's not coming, not coming, but I didn't say a word, most likely working hard at the factory, well already next year he will have gotten himself settled in, I wish he'd at least take Grišiņš with him, I wouldn't have to cross the entire city to take him to the kindergarten myself and then go back to the hospital again, that diarrhoea in the second ward missed his bedpan again, now I have to clean the whole bed, and then she runs, clip, clop, clip, clop, and then she will be there, she'll shout,

'Frosya, Frosya!'

She won't get in to my place, I won't let her in, I hope to god she won't drag someone else with her, thank god, there's no one, she's not there, it's another one, a stranger, a decent woman, talking with Eddy Dārziņš, who is coming home so late? Then, clink, clink, yes, the keys are thrown down, she picks them up and unlocks the door, what a disaster, what are they talking about, everyone has their own worries, that's how it is, is Ulrika back from abroad so soon, perhaps she didn't like it there, I wonder?

Monologue of a Student in the House on the Right Side

A white shirt will be quite impressive, and I've ironed the trousers as well. I need to leave the room clean. The bed made. Here. Right here. And no sign, no explanation. Let them wonder. Let them scratch their stupid heads. Let them try to find out. Let them think. There's no reason to torture myself. The main thing is to have a sure hand, don't be afraid, it's all been decided already. If I don't do it, then I will be a weakling in my eyes for the rest of my life. There's no way back and never will be. Gérard Philipe is already there, John Kennedy is there as well, they didn't do it to themselves, others did them in, but is there really a difference, I'm not doing it to myself either, it's others that have done me in. If I am scared for just a moment, if I am soft for just a moment, then I won't have the strength, the job will remain unfinished, and the next day I will become repugnant to myself for all time.

What do I have to fear? She's already dead. This wedding ride, the cortege, the entourage of cars, actually I was entitled to this wedding cortege. It should have been mine. I should have sat in that sky-blue Volga, next to her, so proud, so stately, she didn't notice me at all, not on the other side of the street near the registry office, or later, when I ran up on the boulevard like a dog, yes, panting like a dog, for two blocks, where she was supposed to drive by. Perhaps she saw me, but it appeared that she didn't notice me, didn't see me, just looked at that tall string bean of a man next to her. Her husband. I was a zero to her, after all that I had said to her, she didn't even want to look at me.

Yes. I needed to be cold, cool, a cunning heart-breaker, I needed to pretend she didn't matter to me, with an unusual English ease, intrigue her with the coolheadedness of a tiger hunter, let her burn with curiosity and attention, only like that! No. Even then it would have been too early. I needed to act my part to the end. Wrap her around my finger and then say it. You don't matter to me. I don't like you. Yes. You're not much of a looker? What? Marry you? It doesn't even cross my mind. I'm good as is. Then she'd crave me, want to make me submit, conquer me. But me? I wouldn't say anything, anything, finally I'd surrender so I could be dragged to the registry office and just on our wedding night confess. 'I loved you for so long! From the first moment I saw you at the institute's party, from the first touch of your arm. From the first scornful glance you threw at me. Once I stood in the rain for three hours under your window.' No. It would be too early even then to confess. Just on my death bed would I dare to confess to my wife. 'You were everything to me!'

Lies. Betrayal.

Romeo, Juliette, that isn't made-up. It was others that interfered in their love, while it was we that destroyed ours.

What can I achieve in this world, full of traitors and pretenders? She's dead to me now. Marrying someone else, that means she's dead. With that tall, swanky, string bean of a guy. How could she make such a poor choice? I don't want to cheat myself unnecessarily, never, I will never meet another girl like that, there is no other, and, if there ever is, and there never will, then I will think of you, Māra, Marusīt, Mātimukiņ, my little blonde mouse, how could you, it was already decided, and us together, and now nothing.

NO ONE ANYWHERE HAS EVER BEEN HAPPY. Everyone has always been unhappy. Why do they live. The unhappy hypocrites. With an unloved job, with an unloved wife? I could also start to pretend myself, but I need you, you.

If reading one's thoughts exists, then you will feel me tonight, you will feel everything that is happening with me, and now I see, you are sitting at the banquet table, with white daffodils in your hair, and, raising a champagne glass to your lips, the guests shout 'Kiss!' demanding the newlyweds kiss, and your husband leans lightly on the back of your dolled-up neck, he kisses you, and you are happy and want nothing other than to kiss forever, and you are slightly dizzy, and your legs become weak, and NO ONE HAS EVER BEEN HAPPY, why did they get married, well, you really don't feel what is happening with me, there is only one path left for me, Romeo is already there, Juliette, Shakespeare himself, Tolstoy, Lenin, Gérard Philipe, John Kennedy, I will also go there.

Will you remember me?

No, never. Maybe once, out of boredom.

And what if?

WHAT?

And what if?

And what if you what? You'll be an idiot. But I will have to think of you, however it doesn't matter, you will be an idiot, you already are an idiot, because you're thinking about it, and then I will remember you as an idiot. No one does that in the twentieth century.

I will.

Because no one is doing it.

Blessed be those who invented windows, those who were the first to cut out those blind eyes in walls, blessed be those! Māra, Marusīte, Mātimukiņ, you run, run, as if a hundred assassins were running to catch you, run, as if all the bloodhounds of the world would be released from their chains, what, what are you doing, my silly girl!

Jauniks's home will not be a refuge for you at all, he is a spiritual bastard, a many-headed human serpent, who has violated you with the blood of his peers, your Husband is a candidate for the gallows, they will find him soon enough, the secret security men never sleep, Māra, Marusīte, don't touch the fence of that scoundrel Eihmanis, don't get your hands smudged up, that's not green paint there, there's blood there!

Run!

Up the steps, even if there are a hundred assassins pursuing you, even if there are a hundred bloodhounds pursuing you, it doesn't matter I will protect you!

The door, I can't unlock the door, the key turns, it turns again, nothing, I push hard on the door with my shoulder, my shoulder makes a thudding sound, I push hard again, keys were invented by a moron, I can't, I can't, and I weep in anger and helplessness, right now, now, I say, I whisper, Māra, are you already at the door, I hear your footsteps, I'll unlock the door, let you in. Don't be afraid. The door is open!

It's not. It's a stranger. Going to the house next door.

Me? Alone?

The Monologue of Asters's Wife Anna

So I have to get up early in the morning, I have to wash the tub, there's always sediment left there, most likely the water's not totally clean, a kind of reddish sediment, there's too much iron or sulphur in the water, you don't know, and then I have to soak the laundry, I have to carry the washing machine from the attic, I'm going to overdo it one day, carrying that washing machine, he never comes to help me, he doesn't have time, he has to be at the garage at six, he doesn't get enough sleep at night either, he has nightmares, this night he hasn't yelled yet, but he surely will at some point, well you don't believe in ghosts, there hasn't been a night when he slept quietly, he should be put in the hospital, or, the building doesn't wake up anymore when he screams now, they're all used to it, everyone's sleeping, yes, tomorrow is off, the day after tomorrow back to the factory to the cauldrons, what's the point of that day off, I have to soak the laundry, the washing detergent is bought, and then I head to the open market, I have to buy meat, you leave later, all the best pieces are already snatched up, you'll be left holding the bag, I have to buy meat, the best is beef, with the bone, one rouble and ten kopecks a kilo, that'll be good, if I get the right piece, I will make bouillon, there'll be something to slurp down, my little Kārlītis will come home starving like always, weak, lanky, and be exhausted from all those schools and cross-country races.

Eddy reads a lot too, and Ulrika is still gone, who will take care of him, calm him, feed him, you can hear every page that he turns in a book, and you can also hear, oh my, goodness me, an old woman, it's not my place to say.

Yes, from those schools and cross-country races, but at least life's easier if you are well-educated, and that Lūcija, nice in every way possible, just she's not right for Kārlītis, not right, such a weak, pale girl, I don't know if it's the fashion or what, that girl doesn't eat, he'll get married to her, and she won't be able to do the housework, or have an idea about family life, and since he was little my little Kārlītis is used to tenderness, attention and being waited on hand and foot, a sensitive child, like he said once in the cemetery, mum, mum, are the dead people cold under the sand?

Then early in the morning I have to get up, soak the laundry, after that go to the market, get meat, milk, butter, cream, cheese, some cottage cheese, one of the cheaper fish, eggs, a lemon, it would be good if I'd get my hands on a fifteen kopeck one, they're the same as one for twenty five, ah, and I also have to get sugar, however you look at it, a ten-rouble banknote won't be enough, everything is so expensive now, in the old money, when you had a rouble, then you had a rouble, now money is melting away without you noticing it, once I came home, I thought, what happened, a pickpocket must have taken my rouble banknote, oh wait, I spent it, in the old money it would have been a hundred for goodness sake, I started to count, I went out just one time to buy groceries, used it up, without buying anything, and it's like that every time at the market, that expensiveness will finish me, on the way, going home, I have to drop by to pay for the rent, the electricity, and don't think that you'll get there without a line, then around noon I will start with the laundry, I won't get there any earlier, at first I will have to put the meat to boil, then the day after tomorrow everything has to be on the shelves, I won't be there for the whole day like usual, at one o'clock maybe I will get to the laundry, noon, what am I saying, how much will there be, six sheets, four pillowcases, where did the blue one disappear to, I most likely stuck it somewhere in the closet, I'll have to look for it, then there will be half a dozen or so shirts, dirty warm clothes that's still not washed, no one will wear that in the summer, I have to wash it, I have to put it out so it sits there, and then it will be autumn again, and then the time will go by from one set of warm clothes to another, and you don't even have time to turn around, everything has already happened, it happened in its own time – youth, and the heat of passion, that dear old thing, soon he'll be screaming his head off, if I knew that the screaming was coming, I could wake him up, my word, I've had fun in my day, but still a person lives from what is, living off your memories is no way to live, and now I don't even have time to take care of my hair, I don't want to stand in line forever to get to a hairdresser, well, then I will have washed everything around six, then I have to scrub the tub, there's also sediment in the tea kettle, but it's drinking water, I guess there's nothing poisonous there, otherwise they would have banned it, then I have to put something on the table for dinner, soup and meat, butter and bread, a cucumber or tin of red peppers, then I have to rinse the laundry out, it will be soaked well, hang it in the attic to dry, then I'll have to take a wet rag and do the floor, I have to wash the dishes, then it will be eleven or so and then that day off is over, I have to go to bed, there's no time to even watch TV, old age isn't far off either.

Ulrika isn't at home, who knows if Eddy is getting frisky. He's like a son to me. I will have to ask him tomorrow if he has some socks to wash, no sense in washing one.

Old age is upon me, there's no time to watch TV, that's how it is, my arms hurt, bringing those heavy bags from the market, and I always have to stand in those lines, my legs are like rocks, and don't even think you can sit in the tram, and you have to move like that the whole day like seaweed, the kitchen, laundry, market, pay for the rent, for the electricity, make something to eat, dishes, clean the house, if you don't do it, who will do it?

Someone went to Eddy's place. With light steps. Well, well, you little rascal. What an indecent boy.

The clothes of my little Kārlītis and my husband need to be mended, sewn, who will you tell this to, who will you complain to. You have to carry on living.

Grīzkalniete's Monologue

Ksh, ksh, ksh, ksh, whish, whish, whish, whish, ksh, ksh, ksh, ksh, and so on.

(Each night Grīzkalniete stuck cotton wadding into her ears, wrapped two towels around her head, with a wool scarf over it, which is why she heard neither Asters's horrible yelling, or Dārziņš's pottering around the flat.)

Monologue of Dračūns's Older Daughter

Mmm, mmm, mm, m.

(Dračūns's older daughter worked in a factory at the stamping press, she pushed a worktable pedal more than one thousand times during the day with her right leg, which is why she slept like a rock at night, and the blood vessels of her right leg showed up on her skin like a strange, secret writing/pattern, Dračūns's older daughter was a true Soviet slave, a workhorse, who pulled the state into communism, but her leg was deformed, and his oldest daughter would be ashamed to show up at the beach next summer.)

Monologue of Dračūns's Younger Daughter

???, ???, ??, ?.

 (She was studying in the last year of secondary school, and no one knew what the younger daughter really thought.)

Monologue of Asters's Son Kārlis

They will awaken, get up, eat eggs, cheese, and cottage cheese for breakfast, lamb soup, pork patties, rhubarb kissel for lunch, and they will eat poppy seed rolls at dinner for better sleep, then they will go to bed and upon getting up once again eat, work, until evening comes, and during their last meal death will cut their throats with a scythe, their children will get up in the morning, eat eggs and cheese for breakfast, lamb soup and pork patties for lunch, poppyseed rolls with tea for dinner, so their sleep is more peaceful and deeper.

I can't do it.

The exhibition was boring. Grey. Pale. There was just one theme in a few variations that was in play – ah, how good we have it finally, finally we have Soviet rule. And then they drone on, our loving rule, that longed-for rule, like for a girl. Are they just simply impotent, spiritually impotent or are they also devilish careerists, who have only business interests in art. Soviet rule, and we're happy? It's great that we finally have Soviet rule! They are going on and on about it for more than twenty years already. Great? If I thought that it wasn't great, I would organise an uprising in Latvia and overthrow that Soviet rule, however I am living under that Soviet rule, I am studying in a Soviet school of higher education, I will be a Soviet artist, so that is also the best proof that this rule is acceptable to me. My life. That is the main proof. But those unending panegyrists, asserters, loudmouths, and blowhards all seemed like frauds to me, who shout 'Look, thief!' just so they can put their hands in another's pocket without abate. Of course, some also shout out of spiritual simple-mindedness, because they have bought into the belief that artists need to work with it. I will show people, not flags, I will show life, not results, I will show passions, not codices. It's all nonsense, the main thing is colours, shapes, lines, and, if that comes to pass in our land, then it will be ours.

I will do that.

My poor father.

What does he see in his dreams, if he screams like that? They must be horrible nightmares, but in the morning he doesn't remember anything. He doesn't remember or he doesn't want to talk about it. Is he unhappy? You can't know what's inside, in his soul. Even he doesn't. The German occupation, the camp, it's good that he stayed alive, and that his health also held up to some extent. He likes Lūcija. Mother doesn't really.

Lūcija.

I did it, first of all I moved the wicker chair, Lūcija sat in it, I sat next to her on the corner of the couch, and the tablecloth had long fringes, I pulled the edge of the tablecloth over our knees, I put my hand on Lūcija's round knee. It was hot. It raced through my joints like electricity, Lūcija also shrunk and froze for a moment. I didn't know if I should take my hand away, she didn't know if she should say something. I didn't take my hand away, but I pressed Lūcija's knee tenderly and firmly, and at that moment she began to talk cheerfully with Alberts, who was sitting on a stool on the other side. I felt that Lūcija's knee was moving away slightly from my hand, so I pressed my fingers in an almost desperate grip, and her knee abated compliantly.

We were among our own here, our entire class, now already our former class, and the merriment came out in full force, and the song 'Here, where the pine forests sway, I am bound with strong ties, here is my homeland, I was born on the banks of the Gauja!'

We all sang, me and Lūcija, and during the song I moved my hand higher and higher on Lūcija's leg, and suddenly my pinky grazed hot, naked velvet skin, and Lūcija shrunk, pushed away my hand, and once again it was like a jolt of electricity ran through my joints, I began to sing even louder and for a moment I put my hand on the table, we sang 'Green hills, broad valleys and many fine wonders', while singing I moved my leg closer and closer to Lūcija's leg, as if accidently touching her and pressed hard against it, we all sang loudly, swinging in our seats as we sang, there was Juris, Valters, Jānis, Alberts, Boriss, Valdis, Anda, Inese, Zaiga, Ilga, Kristīne, Lora, Ilze, Juta, and they sang all of them, swinging in rhythm, and then another song rang out – 'At the Amber Sea, which twists and turns around Courland', and at the next stanza everyone got up on their feet, and had a fun time, we got up on our seats and sang, interlocking our arms, and on the next stanza we got up on the table, and the table was strong and held up, then we finished that song, sat down, and Valdis made a toast, drinking to our health, as if we were some sort of sickly people, now I openly held my hand on Lūcija's knee, she didn't resist, and then Jānis suddenly belted out 'Merry Boys Are Shooting Jews on the Shores of the Gauja Again!' and everyone laughed, and Jānis sang this song in the melody of 'Up the River', he continued singing 'There's only one gun, but a whole slew of Jews!' and Valters shouted 'Throw the Jews in the fire,' almost all of us were Komsomol Youth, but no one told him to stop, everyone was drunk, laughing, some sang along, and then Valters once again shouted 'Jews and communists in the fire!' because the chimney was burning in bright flames and Jānis, drunk, also shouted 'Yes, communists in the fire, are there any communists here?' It seemed like a joke to everyone, and those who saw that he was serious pretended not to hear him, and he seriously shouted it, it was all so wonderfully merry there, I had no intention of standing up, I wasn't even a Komsomol Youth, maybe I was going to make a horrible scene, but those novices were going too far, I got up and yelled 'I am a communist!' and Valters howled, tipping back on his chair, pointing at me with his finger he spilled cognac on and saying 'Moron!' I said 'Well, then throw me in the fire,' and I said it seriously, everyone fell silent, and finally they pretended that nothing had happened, that it was just a joke, finally everything smoothed out somehow, fell silent, we all made up, the drinking continued at full speed, but Lūcija and I snuck out and left. It was night in the city.

We were freezing, so we went into a façade doorway to warm ourselves and stood there till six in the morning, talking about everything, and I only kissed Lūcija a few times, which I am sorry for now. It wasn't a lot. But she didn't want to anymore, we stood under the list of tenants, and on the list there was a peculiar last name, Klakšķis, which meant 'click' in Latvia.

Will I be a prime minister? I doubt it.

I've liked Lūcija for a long time already.

Is she a virgin? What will happen then?

Does she like me?

You can never know!

Asters's Monologue

A small red letter 'a' upside-down rolled out from under the bed, chirping like a chick, and soon after he was joined by a greenish, a little snake coiled up in an 's', then a tiny little gold-coloured hook of a 't' appeared in the middle of the room, which was followed by the letter 'e', placed on its tip like Columbus's egg, with a rumbling 'r' spilling out, and another little snake in the shape of an 's' bringing up the rear of the cavalcade.

The letters assembled themselves into a name, in silence the clock ticked in time

three-fourths, three-fourths,

asters

I couldn't louse this up anymore, interrupt it, I should have gotten up right away, as soon as the 'a' rolled out from under the bed, but now it was too late to defend myself anymore, I should have stood up right away, put on a waltz, only 'An der schönen blauen Donau' could have saved me, or 'Geschichten aus dem Wiener Wald', or 'Künstlerleben', but it was already too late, I wouldn't manage to put on either 'Bei uns z' Haus' or 'Wiener Wald', it was too late, I was damned to look at everything from the beginning to the end, even though I knew very well what will happen, why, why didn't I get up in time, I didn't put on a waltz, I didn't spin the verdict into a maelstrom, until the letters scramble back under the bed, we couldn't be noisy at night, the rhythm of a waltz quickens the heart, the rhythm of a waltz is prescribed for the morning,

one-two-three, one-two-three,

asters.

There was a verdict because I was something a bit more than just a car mechanic. I performed my work well, I didn't get mixed up in politics, but it turned out that also this not getting mixed up in it was politics, and I served my time.

He comes, I have memorised all of the intonations of his voice in my mind, all its nuances, he truly does have a rich voice, he knows how to speak, I already knew beforehand what he would say, but I can't believe what he says, I can't let him in, well, here we go, he is already close, I can make out every wrinkle in his Nordic face, I feel his breath on my cheek.

asters, forgive me this time, you know very well, I'm not guilty.

'You killed them!'

asters, what are you talking about, do I look like a monster, come on, look me in the eyes. Look at me.

'You're a murderer!'

asters, my dear, what are you thinking, you must have heard the rumours, there's a lot being said on the streets, do you think I could have done something like that? What do I get out of that? Come on, let me in this time please, nothing bad is gonna happen!

'This is what you also promised the last time and the time before that you said the same, and the time before that you cried, begged with tears in your eyes, I believed you a countless number of times. I believed you. I let you in. You killed again! I don't believe you. You're a murderer.'

asters, listen to me! Yes, I was, you see, I'm not hiding, denying it, avoiding responsibility. Yes, I killed. But you, you were the one asking me to come in, you let me, allowed me, you were the one who let me in and arranged everything. Isn't that so? Answer me!

'Yes, I did. But I didn't know that you would be killing. I wanted you to be a human being, live like the others. But you killed them. Go away!'

asters! Alright. I'm a murderer. But you believe that I could also be a human being, nothing that is humane is foreign to me, do you think that my conscience has fallen silent? No! It's screaming! Don't you hear how my conscience is screaming? It's screaming 'you're a murderer' with the voices of my victims, it's screaming 'you're a murderer' with the blood of innocent victims. It's screaming 'you're a murderer' with the mouths of unborn children. Victims, innocent people, unborn children? They are all abstractions! Since the beginning of civilisation there have been victims, and there have been executioners. There have been guilty people. Man becomes guilty at birth. The future is an unborn child. When he is born, he will also be guilty. Someone had to kill all the guilty ones. Do you think that it's easy to be a murderer? Destroy another person? Blow out the candle of life? It requires nerves! Nerves and philosophy! Or don't you hear how my conscience is screaming? asters, that screaming is tearing my soul apart. Oh, how horrible I have been, but I wasn't born like that, I was born pure, innocent, I was afraid to kill a fly, and now, looking back at what I've done, the blood curdles in my veins from the horror, I have to tell you, I am forever cured, I've given up my profession, asters, you hear me, in all four corners of the earth, in Paradise, in Hell, in the expanse of the stars, on the diamonds in the entrails of the earth, on all of the spots of the continents I swear, that I have abandoned those bad old ways, I have been born anew in innocence, in love for humankind, and you, asters, will be my best friend, so that I would never be like that again, you will remind me so that I would never repeat that depravity, you will remind me that I was a murderer, but now I am a human being, a human being, that sounds grand! asters, take pity on me, let me in, I can't stand it here, I am cold here outside alone, pushed away by everyone!

The murderer began to sob bitterly.

'I, I don't know, I can't trust you!'

asters, just this time, come on, it's the last time, my eyes are already dry, crying for my sins, I am your eternal friend, even more than a friend, I am in front of you on my knees, I am scattering ashes on my head, and sharp stone bits are making my knees bleed, asters, try to understand me!

'But are you?'

asters, I will always remember this. Always.

'You always address me with small letters!'

ASTERS. A person shouldn't be petty. Forgive me.

'I, I have to talk it over, ask others.'

ASTERS! What do you mean. It's enough for me with your permission, I am being born anew! I will be grateful to you till the end of your life. Be my ally.

AND THE MURDERER CAME INTO THE ROOM AND KILLED MY SON KĀRLIS, KILLED MY WIFE ANNA, I WATCHED, FROZEN IN FEAR.

'You, you promised. To be grateful to me till the end of my life. A friend.'

TILL THE END OF YOUR LIFE, THE MURDERER SAID, AND TWO MASKED MEN WITH FIRM FINGERS HELD MY ARMS AND LEGS. THE MURDERER CAME UP TO ME, RIPPED MY SHIRT APART, WITH A BONY FINGERNAIL SCRATCHED A MARK ON MY HEART, SLOWLY PIERCED ME WITH THE BLADE OF A KNIFE BETWEEN MY RIBS, HE TORE OFF SKIN, MUSCLES, TOUCHED MY HEART.

AAAAAH

Each night he returns, each night

My former lodger Friedrich von Reichenau.

AAAAH!

Dračūns's Monologue

(upon hearing Asters's horrible screaming, Dračūns thought in his sleep)

transitory phenomena leave lasting marks on people's fates, and that is why no phenomenon is temporary, you should throw a slipper over the table three times, here among us, for many years already, because each person's life is transitory, we don't know who he is, Comrade Kumzāns, he's chewing up chicha, which is why he deserves that his life wouldn't be a transitory phenomenon, exactly because that the transitory, chicha, sustenance, spat out into a big pot, filling, juicy, spit-up, broken down, masticated, chewed up, bitten-off, ta, ta, ta, ta

(and he continues to dream that he is riding on a train to the south, where winter is a transitory phenomenon)

The Master's Monologue

Achoo! The front legs will have to be reshoed.

My brother would understand, he's a politician, just as I am. Be dammed, barrels of whirlwinds, lances of lightning, my crazy head, a cold during the summer!

What would my mother say? What would my sister say? At her age? Yes. The bailiff will turn out to be a fine man, he didn't even bat an eye, such a man would sell his mother just so he can attain a higher position. Good. He is suitable. Achoo! However. I myself would be rankled if my bride had been treated like that. Immured. No way! Because the Master has a cold. Achoo. Not because of that, though she is a pagan through and through, but not because of that. Not me. So, is he also rankled? Most likely not. He's cunning. But he keeps quiet. If not him, there will be others.

If he does everything the way it should be done, we will promote him. If not, we will punish him. There must be clarity. Is he with us, or against us. Achoo. We either buy him off, or destroy him. Perhaps I am mistaken, I could repel even the most trustworthy servant with a far-too-strict test. No. He will be trustworthy, he will take this in stride as well. My head is aching. In summer. A cold. God's finger! Not my mother nor my sister can even imagine how difficult it is for us to sow the seeds of faith here. Some must be hewn. To tell you the truth, a soldier and God's servant can have no other task. Everything within me comes from God.

My arms, legs, my shoulders, hips, my bones, veins, flesh, my blood and heart, all my substance, and finally my thoughts all come from God. My cold was also sent by God. His finger. As soon as I become merciful, I will tumble into the water. There can be no greater hint. Achoo. It is through my mouth that God gives his orders, I am not within reach of hell, my commands are of stately importance, I must think about the future, I must think about a faithful bailiff, I must think about a strong, unified state, and one life means nothing here, it is what God wants, and, if I am mistaken, even then I am God's instrument. Achoo. Amen.

And we must shoe his front legs. To sleep. Achoo.

Commander Evian Steele's
Monologue

What a strange people, they even sing at funerals.

'Drink, brother, drink!' Is that a song fit for a funeral? Really? Utter blasphemy. 'Just laugh at everything in life!' What else can you want from them, most likely their only joy in life is to drink their fill, they have not advanced far from the times of Garlieb, when mothers gave children the end of a loaf of bread soaked in spirits, 'Drink and pour, pour, let us forget our cares and troubles!' Well of course, until tomorrow, until tomorrow you will forget them, then once again there will be cares, and trouble, upon your shoulders, utter fools, that is their fate, masonry master Kelle, he asked a high price for his services, covetous and greedy to the core, masonry master Kelle is already preparing the recess in the church wall, but they don't suspect a thing, they are singing and carousing.

You see, old man Rūlis died.

That is what he needed.

In reality we killed him. You see, in this building there was once a telephone, when we occupied the Baltic, we disconnected the telephone. You understand what that means? A telephone means connections. Connections means civilisation. Civilisation means the unity of people. If one person can say something important, significant, or request that someone be quiet for a moment or organise themselves in some other way, or one of some new innovation, ask how one's wife feels after giving birth and whether the rye is turning green, or if the grey mare gave birth to a grey colt, and when that person is twenty, a hundred, or five hundred kilometres away, then that already means something. A telephone unifies people, our aim was to separate people, which is why we disconnected the telephone. Not everyone needs telephones. We are against telephones in general, if they are not in our building. Why do others need telephones? And so we achieved what we wanted. Of course, we were roundly defeated, utterly, but the telephone line was not restored, you see, initially there were wires missing, then they thought that everyone will move to the centre of the collective farm, the telephone poles were stolen one after another, and then, when they decided that each will live in their own home, at least until they die, so let the young do what they want, then it turned out it wasn't worth setting it up. You understand yourself, it's expensive to install a line in such a remote place.

Yes. We take responsibility. We disconnected the telephone. We hurled the communications systems back to the Stone Age. In order that he could say something to a fellow comrade, Rūlis would always head to the centre. While there were still farm horses put up in the house, he was able to go by wagon. Well, then came the tractors, more and more tractors, horses became an item of luxury, they shot old Ancis, shot the other old horses, and ever so gradually liquidated the farm. They moved the remaining colts closer to the centre, and then the only thing left from the old animals the Rūlis family had was a cow. They also had a television, even a washing machine, a good wad of cash in the closet, after the war they had risen quite high, well-established, they had just forgotten one small thing – to fix up the communications systems. It happened at night. All they had to do was call the doctor, call an ambulance, as is known, their medical services are at a high level now, but nothing helped. While the old wife of Rūlis went to the centre, two hours went by unnoticed, the old woman couldn't ride their cow anyway, ha, ha, ha, and some secret allies had already decided that no one needed a telephone, ha, ha, ha, and the horses were all shot, and so

Old Man Rūlis, how old was he at the time, sixty-five, he could have lived longer, till seventy-four years old at least, he was a strong man, even then, while fixing the well, the well frame fell on top of him, but Rūlis wasn't hurt at all, he shook the logs off his shoulders, and crawled up to the light of day safe and sound, he laughed that it wasn't so easy to bury him underground, he hoped to live for a long time, however boastfulness doesn't pay off, his heart was ailing, his heart was already ailing, but no one thought that it was so bad, however the old man kicked the bucket, blew out the candle of life, without being able to see a doctor and modern equipment, yes, what is the point of it all, if communication is at a Stone Age level, ha, ha, ha, and I have confirmed reports, confirmed reports from the doctor himself, that the extra hours decided the struggle in favour of death. In short, the heart attack overpowered Rūlis because there was no telephone at home.

'Drink, drink, brother, drink, just laugh at everything in life!' The wives, their mournful voices slipped into the song, yes, they have good voices, we always killed the men, however the wives remain, the snakes, they continue their kind, the wives, ahem, the men's mighty wives, and it is precisely because of this we are going to immure a wife, and not a husband, a new method, women work like oxen for their husbands, I am not a poet, I am not, the comparisons are cruder as a result, wives blossom like lilies, yes, that sounds much better, that is certainly odd, the men and women are all singing again, they sing at the funeral after centuries of protracted slaughter, most probably a moment of respite has come upon us, look, under the apple trees a couple is kissing, the youth have other cares and concerns in the month of May, and no one suspects a thing, ha, ha, ha!

'Where is my grey mare, where is that crooked osier tree? Where is my broadcloth coat, where is my thousand roubles?' Sing, you blind people, sing! 'All of them left under the counter at the inn! I just hope you haven't left anything under the counter at the inn again! I know you'll sing another song, you will, have you forgotten? 'Let those who want to strike our jugular, fall with a bullet in their brow!' Now you wail 'She is lying on her deathbed, speaking not a word' – that's what you're singing, and that is why Rūlis is gone before his time. He didn't sing the proper way. And nevertheless it's a wonder. Singing even at a funeral, yes, yes, I am telling you!

Master Stonemason Kelle's Monologue

The niche in the wall is already completed, stone put upon stone, I hope that the Order will pay what they promised, if not me, then some other person will snatch that piece of gold away from me, no, my dears, I will not be so stupid, I can brick that girl in, anyway someone will appear, if I refuse, I will be whipped so hard that my skin comes off, if I say no, it doesn't matter, the girl's end is nigh.

Fumes and rumour, both suffocate, everyone knows that an order was given to make the niche the height of a person, a bit smaller than for a man, bigger than for a child, who else will be immured there if not her? Sleep doesn't come at night at all, and so I wander through the courtyard with a beer stein in my hand, looking for a person, a brother in beer, a brother of the beer stein, a brother of the bottle, a brother coming from my people. I rouse Old Lūks from his sleep, the overseer of the horse stable.

'You, drink with me!'

Lūks drank. He was old and didn't dare refuse, otherwise I would have struck him, but my blows were strong.

'You know what will take place in three days? Do you? Do you know or not?'

'You're a pig!' said Old Lūks.

The old man also knew that I was going to snatch that piece of gold out from under someone's nose. I better strike him one so he doesn't dare speak of it. No one can know beforehand, because only then is their rule iron-clad, if no one sticks their nose in the door of those in command. There were still men among the people, those stupid enough and ready, but still men, whose heart still beat in their chest, rather than peas rattling in a pig's bladder. It was only them that were still dangerous, but Old Lūks, he himself was right pig feed, what could he do? He was just shooting his mouth off. No sense in hitting him a second time, he'll be hiccupping after the first one. Of course, he's jealous, the work went right under his nose, just lay there, old man, lay there. Ashes and dust. Thunder and lightning. The Order is as strong as never before, if they were so bold as to do this horrific act. Forgive me, God, that I disparaged your victim! That beastliness with the tearing down of the church walls could not go on for long, it's a miracle that the Order waited so patiently and the guard slept like a rock each night.

They slept? What else could they do, all they could do is sleep, otherwise they would have cut their heads off, they certainly would have been decapitated, either the Order would have cut them off, or those scoundrels, who wrecked the walls at night. If the brothers of the Order are such great men, they should have stood guard a night or two, but no, the locals stood guard, it is clear to everyone, they were vassals, they are in the military not of their own volition, they are newly-baptised little cowards, they don't even know how to recite the Lord's Prayer, they would much rather run back to their forests, they are just waiting for that, for some situation. The whole land is filled with traitors and spies.

Well, they will skin the poor Bremenite alive. And they will come down on him, and he will confess that he added black henbane to the guard's wine, what else could a man say, if the soles of his feet are prodded with a white-hot rod. Each guard has a brother in the forest, a brother-in-law or one of his own people, or some other heathen relative, it's not difficult to arrange everything, speak and afterwards include otherworldly forces. And the disturbances will promptly cease, the girl's soul will bravely guard the wall, as is supposed to be, they will be filled with terror and not lay a finger on the wall.

They say that she's the bailiff's bride, he wants to get rid of her, otherwise he wouldn't have allowed her to be immured. Such a powerful man, almost like the commander himself.

I have crawled into my lean-to, which was set up under the roof, it was dark in here as... hell (may God forgive me, but that's how it was), so it was dark as hell, and a terrible voice said to me:

'Master stonemason Kelle, you have sold your soul, you have sold your flesh, you have disowned your land, you have disowned your father and mother, you have disowned your people. You have been bought with gold, and for gold you will be sold and exhausted by hard work like a yoked ox, and at the end of your life your throat will be slit, like they slit the throat of the black ram. Your flesh will be thrown to the wolves as food, the time will come, your children will wander about, begging for alms. Your father is dead, your mother is dead, and they were both murdered by the lords you are serving. You have disavowed your people's customs, you have disavowed your people's language and only while drunk do you babble a few words in it, you have disavowed your people's beliefs, but experienced no repercussions as a result, we thought that you would return from the path of betrayal, so far you have been spared revenge, but the last stone of the niche in the wall will also be the straw that broke the camel's back.'

Then the voice of consciousness rang out, and I sat up, my stomach tightened by spasms.

'Yes, yes, that is true, I was taken to a foreign land when I was small, severe men raised me, drove the skill of my profession into me with a lash, they taught that there is only one God, they taught one to obey the lords, I was ripped from the teat of my people with force, my faith was beaten out of me by the whip, I am not a traitor, I was forced, my flesh was only scars, and salt was scattered on top for good measure, my soul was only scars, they threatened you with the horrors of hell, I don't know what a nation is, I don't know what

116

Thunder is, I don't know what freedom is, I just wanted to survive, stay alive at any price, I didn't want them to skin me alive like that man, that Bremenite, I am small, I want to leave, which is why I needed money, money, gold, gold, small, I am small, small,

and, after throwing up a good part of the beer I had drunk in the straw, I finally fell asleep.

Bailiff Dārziņš's Monologue

Could we free ourselves from the Order's supreme rule and establish our own state? If so, then only in cooperation with other peoples, but the Lithuanians were currently fighting the Rus', the Rus' were currently battling the Tatars, while the Estonians were pillaging in northern Livonia. We were isolated. How would bearing our teeth early help if it causes harm to our mutual cause? It would be better to draw back, wait it out patiently, and strike at the right time. What would I receive as a result?

The title of land marshal, respect, power.

What would I lose?

Ulrika, a clean conscience, freedom.

What is freedom actually? A word. This word will be banned in every land. If someone writes 'Let Freedom Live!' on the wall, they will be sent to the gallows at once, because 'there is already freedom in our land, so he must have meant the freedom of his neighbour, but my neighbour is an enemy.' Freedom? I will be free when I will be on the summit of power, when I will scoop up in my hands all the strings in this world of puppets, I will be free among my circle, my narrow circle, where I will be recognised by my own people, I will greet the Order's great warriors in the informal 'you' form, with the Master as well, and then I will speak. Thereandthere somanyandsomany people are boiling a doe in clarified butter, and I will decide, if it should be left so, thereandthere somanyandsomany people will chew on bitter chaff bread, and I will decide if it should be left so, thereandthere somanyandsomany people have had their tongues ripped out, and I will decide, if it was done correctly, the sweet seat of power will embrace me, my staff, my title, respect and power attached to a secure place, my heart will slide down to the bottom, the mind will roam to the heights, my head pure, my judgement unbiased, I will rule enlightenedly, there will be much to do, truly, ruling is the work of a jeweller, you have to tighten the screws at just the right time so the structure doesn't collapse (no, you have to be an all-purpose handyman), let off some steam, so the boiler doesn't bubble up over the top and burn you, there you have to caulk the cracks, so fresh air doesn't get in and a bad smell doesn't emit from there, on the one hand smile, and on the other hand whip, the suppleness of the noose and the ruthlessness of the hangman should be used, he will kill publicly, but the other around the corner, correct, Marshal Dārziņš, now you are ours, tighten, fill the holes with pitch, don't be shy, see, they're not grumbling, not rebelling, because it was once said – each people has the government they deserve. Live, rule, be happy, Dārziņš, you have a grand castle, bodyguards follow your every step, horses at your disposal, first-class servants, we will obtain a nice woman for you as well, of course, not from your people, you will live like a king, free, all-knowing, every now and then striking the people on the back of the neck with a sword, don't let them think of straightening out their hunched back, let them always watch the land, let them think of land, let them work, plough, sow, harrow, cut, give bread to us, to you, don't let them raise their eyes up, examine, what, for whom, why, where, from what, how much, it's a peasant's way of thinking, but you, Dārziņš, you will live like a king, occasionally saddle up your battle steed, put your armour on, you will have to fend off the Order, the Rus', then the Lithuanians will come to rip us apart, the Samogitians will rise up, they will all need to be suppressed in a timely manner.

And the Order's servant Dārziņš will be killed in some battle. And nothing more. It will be written upon your grave:

BOUGHT CHEAPLY

Pangs of conscience? I have bowed for ten years, crawled on my stomach, hid, risen higher and higher, believing that I will remain pure, unsullied, that at the end I will play my trump card, and now I see that power is simply a net, nothing more. The sweet taste of power is tempting. I will die in a horrid stench, in slimy manacles. And what will I have attained? *Homini necesse est mori.* And it will still be standing there.

BOUGHT CHEAPLY

Ulrika, that's what you will think of me, as you go on your last walk, that is what my friends will think of me, that is what my war comrades the Samogitians will think of me, that is what all the honest people will think of me. What do I care about the honest people, what do I care about my comrades-in-arms, my friends, just Ulrika, my great love, well, instead I will receive my silver armour, the staff of power, new friends, a new love, I will be allowed to see foreign lands.

But no one will become friends with you, knowing you are a traitor, no one will drink with you without apprehension, no one will love you without furtive fear.

And so what? I will drink with those very same traitors, my friends will also be traitors, my lovers will follow me. *Hodie mini, crass tibi*[5], enough, enough, you are a clever man, Master, you are clever, only you are wrong, thinking that I will sing *Te Deum laudamus*, there are other songs, and I myself am from another time, I have seen much, this trick will not work on me, I have travelled here through the centuries in time's veiny palm in order for you to pay up, now you have given me a pretext, you let me leave, you prepared everything, yes, yes, no one knows if I am a Latvian, a Russian, a German, a Swede, a Dane, a Lithuanian, an Estonian, a Pole, a Czech, a Finn, however I have put down roots among these people, these people have raised me, educated me, fed me, I have been educated too well, experienced too much to befoul myself

---

[5] Latin for 'My turn today, yours tomorrow'

with betrayal and at the same time those many people that have believed in me – 'Let those who want to put us under the yoke, fall with a bullet in their brow!'

And if I lose? What then?

Part Three

The Twilight Hour

1

Having gone to the bathroom, I took the unknown woman's shirt, her bra, slip, tights, dress, I looked for a long time as I searched for her panties, I couldn't find them anywhere, neither on the floor, nor behind the tub, then I brought the clothes to the room; her coat and shoes were already there in front of me. Apparently she didn't have anything else with her, perhaps these rags were the only things that belonged to her.

The Twilight Hour

2

What belonged to me?

One good Belgian suitcoat with the brand of a company from Antwerp that was worth one hundred and seventy roubles, a pair of trousers from inexpensive wool material, a well-worn suit jacket, worth twenty roubles, a winter coat, made in Bulgaria; to be more precise – it was a midseason coat, with a velvet collar, black, the original price one hundred and forty roubles, now even the pawn shop didn't take it anymore, however I hoped to wear it for two more years. I also owned ten white shirts, one grey shirt, a checked shirt, a black shirt, I owned a beret, a rabbit fur hat with earflaps, two pairs of leather gloves, three pairs of shoes, a pair of winter boots lined with soft material, a leather jacket, two robes, six duvet covers and sheets, two chequered wool blankets, three chairs, bookshelves, a small gas stove, a kitchen table, a television-radio unit, a mat, an electric leg warmer, about two thousand books, two paintings, one gifted by an artist named Ulpe, the other I bought at a second-hand art shop as a work by Matvejs Tīts[6], afterwards it turned out to be a forgery. I owned six soup plates and as many dinner plates, two small pots, a frying pan, a set of knives and forks for six, teaspoons and tablespoons made of nickel silver with the engraved inscription 'stainless', three champagne glasses, another dozen glasses of various sorts, sunglasses with sea grey lenses, made by Zeiss, a pair of tennis shoes, one pair of warm longjohns, eight

---

[6] Matvejs Tīts (1913-1978) was a Latvian painter.

pairs of underwear, imported from Arabia, twenty ties, both bought and gifted, a Moskvitch, the oldest model, purchased for seven hundred roubles, if you convert it to the new money, shaving accessories, two dozen handkerchiefs, empty bottles, a nickel-plated corkscrew, vases, a pen knife, an umbrella, a raincoat, tobacco boxes, pipes, pipe cleaners, a mirror, an iron, twenty eggs, a jar of horse-radish, a loaf of bread, cheese, a pack of tea, half a kilo of coffee, a kilo of sugar, half a bottle of sour cream, half a litre of milk, a kilo of macaroni, bouillon cubes, a jar of pickled cauliflower and four hundred roubles in bank savings.

I was rich. I was Croesus.

What did Croesus own? I don't know.

Ulrika owned almost nothing. I got to know Ulrika at the pawn shop, as she was pawning off some worthless ring with a fake diamond, receiving five roubles for it.

However, if Ulrika listed the things that belong to her, my name would be in first place on the list. She told me that once. I am a thing which belongs to Ulrika. Since I belong to Ulrika, she can't belong to me. The clothes, dishes, vehicles, we wear things, we eat, we drive, we sell work, we buy things, we work for the sake of things, we philosophise for the sake of things, we work again, work our butts off, grit our teeth, fight tooth and nail for, better, better, live more prosperously, more, we need more things, we sell arms, legs, brains, we sell time, we buy things to replace things, we sell will, nerves, we sell health, things surround us on all sides, because the more things we have, the sunnier the future will be, we have to produce, we have to hurry to buy more, sell, wait, wait, when finally we will be swimming in prosperity, carpets, cars, champagne, owners love things, but things never love their owners, the wheel turns, you pull out the winning ticket, everything gets muddled up, changes, owners turn into things, things turns into owners, we topple the tsar, God, things, we construct things, sweet is the bondage of things, to be a glass, that your lord drinks from, to be a car and take your lord around in a metal stomach, it's sweet to be sugar, which dissolves in a cup of tea, which flows into a lord's stomach, it's heroic to be a lord's soles, to protect the tender soles of his feet from the hard stone teeth of the cobblestone, it's wonderful to be a lord's gloves, to protect his fine hands from life's dross, it's an honour to shine like a medal on your lord's chest, it's flattering to be a collarette, to hold a jelly-like double chin at bay, the wheel turns, things become owners, owners become things, become people again, they are happy for a brief moment, they are horrified for a brief moment, make a decision, don't carry it out, but the wheel just turns, you pull out the winning ticket, unneeded things are destroyed, they don't produce thinking things, they could become dangerous, the Union of Soviet Socialist Refuse grinds them up again in another way. Everything is solved in such a simple way.

P. S. I also own a suitcase, two stools in the kitchen, around one tonne of coal in the cellar, ski boots, slalom skis with ski poles, ten or eleven pairs of socks, old coins, a few odds and ends, small coffee grinders. And surely a few other things, which I have forgotten to mention here.

The Twilight Hour

3

The unknown woman slept, fast asleep, even occasionally snoring. Sleep at the twilight hour is the deepest. I put on my shoes, put on my leather jacket, and locked the door behind me.

The Twilight Hour

4

There was about half an hour left until sunrise, a crimson red arc of clouds shone in the grey tin-like sky, my (clicking) steps echoed in the morning silence, green birch leaves, dew on the fences, and I came out at the shore of the lake near the boat dock, and the sand muffled the sounds of the steps. I walked back and forth along the lakeshore, inspecting in detail the two-coloured blue and green boats, I walked along the small jetty and then back, I examined the embankment, I didn't see one footprint in the sloping sandbank, the water had risen higher that night, it had licked it clean with the tongues of the waves. While walking back, I noticed a black object on the door of the boat dock shed. As I got closer, I saw a woman's purse. I picked it up and opened it. The outer pocket contained lacy underwear. It was more than a document, because I knew who the bag belonged to. Cautiously, taking it with two fingers, I took out the underwear, in the purse there was also a flat face powder container, lipstick, two crumpled handkerchiefs, eight roubles, a three-by-four-centimetre photo of a young man, used tram tickets, and four keys on a keyring. No documents.

Why was she running? It was a mystery to me, because I still didn't know anything. If someone had tried to rob her, it doesn't matter how, for things or for dignity, the bag wouldn't be here anymore, because thieves of honour love things just as much as they love robbing someone else's dignity. They would have at least taken the money. Maybe no one attacked her, she was walking near the lake at night, caught sight of the waves' fatal sprint to the shore, a desire to throw herself in the lake was thrust upon her, to sink, to disappear in the waves, sometimes a person is overcome by such irrational thoughts. At this point I started to laugh, as unbelievable as it all sounded. My little trip hadn't been in vain, at least I had found something, although the general picture had not become any clearer, I had not come any closer to the truth.

The Twilight Hour

5

I still hadn't reached Jauniks's building, when I heard the door being closed, and the head of that mysterious citizen flashed on the path in the garden. Another head appeared alongside it, and those heads passed the gooseberry bushes, apple trees and plum trees ever closer to the gates, and I still had about ten metres to reach them when the gates opened up and my neighbour to the right, a young student, came out of the garden. The gates closed, almost simultaneously with the clink of the hook, and the head of the mysterious citizen Jauniks passed back along the plum trees, apple trees, lilacs, and gooseberry bushes.

'Ah,' the student said. 'Out for a walk? So early?'

'You are as well, I see.'

'Yes,' the student replied absentmindedly and asked me to go along with him.

'You're probably wondering,' he asked.

'What about?'

'You see, I went to that guy's place,' he gestured with a wave of his hand at Jauniks's house.

'Do you know him?' I asked with interest.

'No, no,' the student answered as if he was even a bit frightened, 'I don't know him.'

We had arrived at the front of my building. I was getting ready to say goodbye, then the student suggested that we walk a bit more. I thought he would want to tell me something, which is why I agreed, and we continued walking.

'What do you know about him?' the student asked.

The same that everyone knows, gossip, rumours, bad liver, and nothing more.

'I was in a strange mood yesterday,' the student said, 'otherwise I wouldn't have by any means gone over there. I thought that I won't get past the gates, the angry dog will attack my legs, the gates, of course, were locked, but I rang, and then he let me in, no more than five minutes went by, before he let me in.'

'He let you into his house?'

'Well, yes.'

What did you want from him?'

'He asked the same question. I said that I wanted to talk with him. He seemed to bristle at the thought, I thought that he was going to let me have it and start swearing at me, call his dog on me, but he asked who I was. I said that I was a nearby neighbour. Well, then come in. I noticed that something flashed across his face, something like satisfaction, if you could say that, but I still didn't know why. We went into his living room. He said:

'Is this your handiwork?'

He pointed to the corner. A big dog was sitting on a blanket there, his tongue hanging out, panting, his sides sunken, it was clear he was in agony. I was covered in a cold sweat, the situation had taken a turn for the worse.

'How did that happen? What happened?'

'Someone poisoned him. Is this your handiwork? What do you say?'

Bristling angrily, he looked at me. He thought that I had given his dog poison and how I had come to confess.

'No.'

'No. Of course not! So why did you come here in the middle of the night then?'

I was shaking in my boots, I apologised and wanted to leave, but he stopped me and said I should say what I had wanted to say. I became irritated. There was nothing else left to do. I gathered myself and spat it out, I thought, whatever happens happens. I said that I had heard all sorts of gossip and horror stories about him, I had come to see how much of it was true and how much of it was lies.

'What gossip, what horror stories?'

'That you led operations. You compiled lists.'

'Young man, have you ever served time in jail?'

'No.'

'Well, I wouldn't wish it upon you. I wouldn't wish it. But I, you see, spent the best years of my life in prison. You can't understand that. You're studying, everything is served to you on a platter, everything's for free, both education, as well as medical services, spas, the future belongs to you, and you can't even imagine something like that. Young man, can you imagine the prisons during bourgeois Latvia?'

'I can't.'

'Correct. You can't! But I spent the best years of my life in a forced labour prison. Do you read books? Do you know what a forced labour prison means?'

'I do.'

'You don't know a damn thing! What can you, young people, know about it. Your minds are full of mush, you know too little of life! Just wait.'

He went into the adjoining room. I heard him pick up the telephone, I thought that he was going to call so they could come and arrest me.

'No, it's not better. No. Not at all. His breathing is fast, Yes. Yes. Yes. Thank you. I did everything. As you instructed. Ok. That's unfortunate. That's unfortunate. Thank you. Goodbye.'

He had called his dog's veterinarian. I looked around the room.

The only thing there was a single chair near the blanket with a dying dog. There wasn't any other furniture. Near the wall hung muzzles, a few photos. The dogs depicted in the photos looked at me energetically, on the floor were two food bowls. I still didn't quite understand, and then it occurred to me that this was the dog's room. His dog lived here. His wife, children, and relatives slept on the top floor. I gathered up the courage to ask the next question.

'And so you're taking revenge on everyone?'

He didn't hear me, he went to his dog, bent over, stroked his pedigree head, and said: 'Kob, little Koba, Kob, Kob, there, there!'

The dog's scent had seeped into the walls, floor and ceiling.

'How did that happen?'

This time he heard me and replied. In the evening, around nine, Koba began to scrape his paws against the outside door, he wanted inside, he wasn't let in, he began to whine and howl, normally the dog would want to come inside only after eleven, and then Jauniks realised that something bad had happened. The veterinarian pumped his stomach, cleaned out his intestines, gave him a shot of antitoxins, but it seemed that nothing had helped.

'Young man, you said I'm taking revenge? I'm not taking revenge, I am carrying out the will of the people.'

'But how do you know what the will of the people is?'

'I have been up since ten in the evening here, I have been sitting and watching, how my dog is dying, but you aren't ashamed at all to come at night and ask me loaded questions! Don't you have a conscience, young man? Do I look like a monster? Do you think that I could sleep peacefully at night if my hands were soiled? What do you want to hear from me? Some sort of penance? There aren't any sins of that that sort upon my shoulders. If I have sinned, I would receive my punishment.'

'Maybe they didn't punish you because then too many people would have to be punished?'

'That's not for you to decide!'

'But for whom then?'

'Only the people can decide that.'

'But aren't I "the people"?'

Then I felt that I had said too much. Who knows what Jauniks would have answered, but the dog wheezed in a strange way, he hurried to the dog, then to the telephone.

Yes. There was foam around his mouth. Quick, soft, barely palpable. Deep, noisy and uneven. Yes. Yes. Yes.

He injected the dog with medicine, but it didn't help, and after a minute or two Koba stopped breathing.

And Jauniks? He began to cry. He whispered 'My dog, my dog!' I understood that I had come at the entirely wrong time, expressed my opinion at the entirely wrong time, said goodbye, he also didn't try to stop me, he asked me to say my address, name and last name, he supposedly knew that I had poisoned his dog, I had come to revel in the throes of death, they would investigate it all anyway. He accompanied me to the gate. What was going to happen to me now?'

The Twilight Hour

6

'But you didn't poison his dog, did you?' I asked the student.

'It didn't even cross my mind,' he replied.

'Nothing will come of it. Most likely Jauniks isn't stupid, his initial sorrow will pass, he'll understand that you didn't go to his place to gloat. Well, goodbye then.'

'But what do you think about all of this?' the student asked, being persistent.

'It's the same thing as poking a dead dog with a stick. You'll just get flies up your nose.'

We said goodbye. It was clear that the student was sorry that he had been open with me. I thought to myself that the student was naïve, perhaps even a simpleton. What's the point of such attempts to fix the world? You can't fix the past. You can only look ahead. I felt refreshed and relaxed. That short walk had reinvigorated me.

The night was as good as over, there was just a short while until sunrise, a lustrous ploughshare of clouds broke through the greyish tin sky, there, up above, the sun was already shining.

The Twilight Hour

7

When I returned, the unknown woman was still sleeping. I settled down for a nap in the deep, well-worn armchair, where in his time Mr. Dārziņš had lounged about so gladly, and I smoked my pipe with aromatic tobacco. Footsteps could be heard in the hallway, as Asters was getting ready for work. The building was sleeping in a morning drowsiness, it was dreaming its last dreams, the ringing of the nickel-plated alarm clocks would be belting out in the rooms in half an hour to an hour, wrest the renters from non-existence, from sleep, from warm and comfy beds, throw them into the haste of the day, the city's buzz, the anthill of humanity. Having smoked my pipe, I stretched with delight, a pleasant weariness fell upon my eyelids. The sun rose at five hours and twenty-seven minutes.

Sunrise

1

A fog still covered the fields, and the sun had just risen, dew sparkled on the road like silver chain mail, as ten carts drove at a slow pace from the forest and approached the castle. The wheel axles greased with tar groaned pitifully, with each cart pulled by two heavy yoked and snorting oxen.

'Hey-ho! Hey-ho!' the peasants yelled, and hemp whips cracking flew over the oxen's backs, more to scare them than to cause pain.

The guard in the tower blared a signal of approachment, and the officer on duty went in to Commander Evian Steele to inform him that the peasants were approaching the castle. The head of the guards came from the commander's chamber in a slow, lazy gait, so it was clear he must have received an order to let the drivers bring the stones over the castle bridge. A moment later I saw the brothers, knights, and the commander going into the prayer chapel.

The castle stood in an open plain, any attack would fail, because the guards would be able to close the gates on time, but we had neither a battering ram, nor the ability to surround the castle for a long period of time.

There were six men lying in each cart, covering themselves with shields, with a layer of stones piled on them. I myself tried out lying down in the cart, they were not very large throwing stones, and lying under a shield didn't appear to be too difficult. The ten carts were prepared in a similar fashion, the best warriors had camouflaged themselves in them, and then from these carts they had to drive to the castle in the light of day, the guards would let the carts over the bridge and into the inner courtyard without second thought, it was just five peasants, each driving two carts, they wouldn't raise the slightest suspicion. The road to the nearest forest was one hourglass long, if the horses went at full speed, and then these sixty men they would need to hold their ground at any cost, and not allow them to close the gates and raise the drawbridge, as a brigade of riders hiding in the forest would rush in.

I had gotten up, already before the sun I had instructed my most faithful people, how it had always been foreseen to use Latvian soldiers in the most difficult labour, in the unloading of stones from the carts, although according to regulations they were viewed as fully fledged garrison members and hard labour was not a part of their duties. Yesterday the Holy Father had come to me and requested that I personally organise the unloading of the stones, not suspecting at all how much I had awaited this proposal. After haggling a bit, I of course agreed.

The carts groaned pitifully near the castle gates, the heavy drawbridge dropped slowly, and, look, already the first pair of yoked oxen dug their hooves into the bridge.

The brothers, knights, and commander were just going into the castle's small prayer chapel to call upon the Lord their God, the mercenaries were having breakfast in the grand hall, the moment was more than favourable.

I turned the hourglass upside down, and soon after the warning signal soared on the flagpole.

The stones rattled and flew apart in the first cart, and the stones in the other carts also flew up into the air at once, the men leapt onto the ground, their shields clanged. Some of the people fell on the ground straight away, not because they had been felled by weapons, but because their limbs had become totally numb after lying in that uncomfortable position. A moment later they got on their feet again and once again fell. The others were already in swordfights with the surprised guards, but I, standing on a high platform in a corner tower, only saw those who had fallen and gotten up, and cursed, unable to participate in the battle, they were four or five men, the rest were already fighting the guards, but I, standing on a high platform in a corner tower, only saw those four or five men, and it truly would have been humorous, such large, powerful, angry men, but they jumped around like jesters on a string, it truly would have been humorous if the situation hadn't been so tragic, the guards from the opposite corner tower, the commander's men were positioned there, shot arrow after arrow, and my four to five men with their numb limbs fell one after another, and then the guards also stopped shooting and turned to their swords, their time had come to die, and they died earlier than the hourglass had the chance to empty halfway.

A band of mounted soldiers rode in with the distant rumble of hooves, however it seemed that the horses were galloping unusually slow, the entire mass glided backward more than forward, the riders wouldn't reach the castle in time, and I climbed over three dead bodies; it was the guards of this tower lying there, the commander's men, and I prepared to go down the steps as the messenger ran upstairs.

'It's all over,' he informed me, 'the guards have fallen, the commander together with the brothers and knights have locked themselves in the castle's small chapel.'

'And the mercenaries?'

'They were not hard to deal with, they were having breakfast without their armour, without weapons, and they were killed over their food bowls. Around twenty of our men perished.'

Over the messenger's shoulders I saw the castle courtyard, I saw our men and then a sudden disarray in their ranks, a disorderly movement backward, and then like a whirlwind a wedge formation with about nine brothers and led by two knights appeared, as

Commander Evian Steele flew into the ranks of the soldiers like a whirlwind, his white cloak with a black cross fluttered behind the commandry, fluttering to the left with each strike to the right side, and fluttering right with each strike to the left side, and the black cross had been stained with numerous red crosses. The commander fought off the enemy's blow, the cloak fell behind him, almost wrapping around his legs, and the commander jumped out ahead, stabbed with his sword, and his cloak stretched out straight, and Evian Steele leapt over the corpse, his cloak grazed a dead body, and the blood left yet another red mark on his cloak. It was a wonder that Evian Steele did not entangle himself in that flag of death, that he did not stumble, he used the sail-like cloth of his cloak in a virtuoso manner to balance himself.

I saw all of this over the shoulders of the messenger. I saw how the knights leading the wedge formation of brothers rushed to the gates to raise the bridge, I saw how my lightly-armed men were retreating and someone took my heart in their hot hand. Evian Steele shot a glance up, and caught sight of me.

'Eduards,' his voice rang over the curses, groans, a deathly wheezing, and the clanging of swords and armour.

'Eduards! We need you. We are in danger!'

The swift attack quelled near the gates. My men gradually pushed the brothers back. One knight fell.

'My glove,' I called to the messenger, and no less than five heartbeats later I had rolled up the glove, took aim, threw it at him, and hit the commander in the face.

'Treason!' Evian Steele shouted.

More than half of the hourglass had flowed, one could clearly hear the rumbling of the hooves, one could make out the snorting and whinnying of some horses, the commander's armour clinked in the tower passage, and like an arrow from a bow, Evian Steele burst into the small tower rampart.

I did not worry about Ulrika. Just as the stones began to fall from the carts, two of my best archers had stationed themselves at the end of the hallway, having shot both guards with arrows, and taken up their places, and with the heavy, massive doors as a cover, they were both able to hold out against an entire band of soldiers and pierce through more than ten attackers with arrows, while they ran through the long hallway. Ulrika was safe.

'Get away,' I cried out to the messenger, who attempted to protect me. 'Get away. And then downstairs.' And then a heavy blow fell upon my sword, and after that was followed by a string of blows from the left and the right and disengage strikes from below, and lance-like jabs straight from the front, and feints, which I had to judge correctly, and horrendous, brutal frontal attacks, where you used not only your sword, but also your weight as well as your armour together with a parrying dagger in your other hand. Evian Steele pulled back to create distance and made two cross blows above my head, I could under no circumstances block the blade of his sword, otherwise the blow would slide and catch my shoulder, thus one would do well to avoid it. Much to his detriment, Evian Steele had once taught me all the finer points of swordfighting, elucidating upon the meaning of why one should use force and the necessity of feints, trained my reactions to the point of them becoming automatic, back in the day he had put his best effort into making me a worthy soldier for the Order, and in my way I had strived from my whole heart in order to attain the best I could from the commander's experience.

The rumble of the galloping cavalry grew louder, and the commander suddenly jumped back a safe distance from me, dashed to a hole in the wall so he could see what was happening on the road. I also dashed to the other hole in the wall, this was where the matter of life and death was being decided, which is why we briefly stopped our duel. The cavalry galloped up a slope, and suddenly the drawbridge's chains began screeching and the bridge slowly began to slide up, and the first horse tumbled into the moat with his rider. Behind him fell the second horse, but the rider was able to grab the end of the bridge and was left swinging there for a moment, until he flung his legs over the edge and crawled up, with the entire bridge slowly sliding towards the mouth of the gate. The ranks were thrown into disarray from the sudden stop in their mad dash, the cavalry was twisted into a vortex, and the horses piled on top of one another, slid down on all fours up to the edge of the moat, but the bridge slid up unrelentingly, and a single soldier, balancing himself, was able to run past the massive chain, the blade of his sword gleaming in his hand. In the gate curses could be heard, as well as the clanging of swords. Evian Steele once again threw himself at me, but already with my first blow I pierced his chest with my weapon.

Sunrise

2

I had most likely dozed off, because suddenly I was woken up by a strong knock at the door. I opened my eyes, I saw that the clock showed half past seven, the room was filled with sunlight, the unknown woman was still sleeping, with her head covered with the blanket, and, having not quite woken up yet, I shouted:

'Come in!' To be more precise, it was my reflex to say it like that, and it worked impeccably this time too.

Revolver Mick came in.

It's alright. I got up calmly, I went up to him, stuck out my hand.

'It's good I found you at home,' Mick said. 'Sorry, is your lady still sleeping?' He looked towards the couch. The woman groaned, freed her head from the cover, looked at us for a moment with wide, sleepy eyes, then once again hid her head under the blanket.

Mick stepped back, raised both his hands in a gesture of repulsion, mouthing a big 'O' in the wry look on his face, then pursing his lips and whispering 'Shhh', closing his eyes, as if saying 'I have not seen a thing, I swear!' and upon finishing this fooling around, said:

'Where can we talk?'

'Let's go to the kitchen.'

The house was silent. In the first-floor kitchen Dračūns and his wife were having breakfast right at that moment, the respectable lady was having breakfast in her room, the lonely mother Frosya had already left to take Grišiņš to the kindergarten, the married Tomiņš couple were already at work, Dračūns's oldest daughter had already pressed the stamping press pedal about three hundred times, while their youngest daughter was reading a newspaper at the tram stop, Urka was smoking his morning cigarette, Lyolya was still sleeping, their son Jura was going to school all while messing around, both of the Tomiņš children were going to a different school. The second floor was also silent. Asters was at work, his wife Anna had gone to the market, Grīzkalniete had still not come out of her room, but Asters's son Kārlis normally left precisely at half past seven, and Revolver Mick most like had passed by him in the stairwell.

Revolver Mick was a handsome man in the prime of his life, with the right facial features, short cropped hair, the mouth of a cynical epicurean. His real name was Miķelis, however during his second year at university he had gotten that nickname. Mikus had fallen in love with an unusually pretty blonde from the physics and mathematics faculty, of course it couldn't have ended well, the girl ended up liking another guy, and she gave Mikus the cold shoulder. Mick didn't show up for lectures for three days. On the evening of the fourth day, while heading home, we noticed a figure hunched in the corner of the vestibule, amazingly similar to Mikus, the collar of his grey rain jacket covering half of his face, a hat pulled down over his forehead.

It smelled of blood there, which is why we asked:

'What are you planning to do?'

Our gut feeling had not failed us, because Mick, looking around suspiciously, pulled an eighteenth-century pistol from the inside pocket of his coat.

'One barrel for him, the other for her!' Mick said.

You could never know when Mick was joking, and when he was speaking seriously, once at a seminar he expounded the stupidest drivel with the most serious look on his face, however it was such politically correct drivel that the teacher didn't dare interrupt him, because he understood very well that Mick was waiting precisely for that.

Mick had filched the pistol from a museum, the pistol was loaded, and we needed to lure him to a beer hall, it would be just then that we'd have the chance to disarm him. I don't believe that Mick would have shot it, no one believed that, even though there was a percussion cap on the nipple, however Mick claimed that he would have. Boom, boom, and it's over!

He was expelled because of poor grades. For a time he worked in a morgue, no one was ever surprised by that, you could expect anything from Mikus; he visited me several times, telling me his horrible experiences in the preparation room with the dead bodies, then he disappeared and now, after a good many years, he appeared almost unexpectedly at my place at such an early hour of the morning. His proposition was bizarre.

'I want to borrow money from you,' he said.

'How much do you need?'

'Five thousand.'

It didn't sound serious.

'Alright, alright,' I laughed, 'just wait a sec, I'll write you a cheque.'

'I'll be honest with you,' Mick continued, 'I want to buy a car. A Volga.'

'Go right ahead,' I said, 'just don't drive it into the ditch.'

Then Mick explained the real reason behind his favour. The thing was supposedly simple. He needed to go to a notary he knew, the notary would draw up a loan document, stating that I had given Mikus five thousand, and Mikus, of course, wouldn't take the money, because he had plenty of money, he was swimming in it, he just couldn't use that money.

'Why can't you use it?'

Apparently Mikus's standing in society had improved, he had supposedly worked in a few positions, he had also been in the brotherly Soviet republics, but his last job had been in Latgale, on some collective farm, of course, in the position of chairman. Then he supposedly had worked according to his conscience, within a year the collective farm improved from being in last place in the region to the third-worst, but then at last it turned out that Mikus had become really fond of the collective farm's pigs, and at the end of the year more than ninety pigs had disappeared. Mikus admitted that he had become fond of a third of a pig each day. Then those pigs disappeared for some mysterious reason, but no one could pin it on Mikus because he had covered it up so well, then he was happily released and with the help of God returned to Riga, having supposedly lived there for some time, but not knowing what he could do with the pig money; he supposedly had other savings, but he said he was definitely being followed, God, what kind of country was this, where you can't even spend money, it was hell, not life, he would have been better off living in America.

'In America you, my friend, would have been put in Sing Sing long ago,' I said to Mikus. 'Our country is the only place in the world where swindlers are treated humanely.'

'I didn't steal, I just took what I was entitled to. Because everything belongs to us, just we don't have everything in our hands. I only took what I was due from the state.'

'Didn't you get paid bonuses?'

'Of course. But what was needed were extra bonuses. I was an honest worker. What was good for the collective farm, was also good for me.'

'Mikus,' I said, 'and if I need to get that money back I didn't give you?'

'Come on, you're an honest guy.'

'Mikus, you need to know my principle,' I said. 'My principle is to not get involved anywhere. I wouldn't even think of giving you money that way.'

'But you're not giving me money, instead I will give you a little wad. I just need the paper to say that you've given it to me.'

'You're a good guy, Mikus, but it's just not right.'

Mikus was silent. Then he said:

'You can get all involved with whores, but when it comes to helping out a friend, you'd rather sit on your hands.'

'What?'

'You know who that girl is you have on the couch?'

'You know her?'

'Three roubles for a night. Did you pay her more?'

'She gives it to me for free,' I replied.

'I see. Well, just watch out that you don't get the clap.'

Mick was starting to become obnoxious. Now I could tell him to scram, to leave my, ahem, ahem, luxurious flat, but would that change anything? I wouldn't be a better person, or Mick a worse one. Moreover, I had found out a thing or two.

'Well, forgive me, take care of yourself.'

'See you and the next time don't be so belligerent,' Mick said, saying goodbye.

When I went back in my room, the unknown woman had woken up, was lying down, stretched out, with the blanket to her chin.

'Good morning.'

'Good morning.'

'Where are my clothes?'

'On the chair. Look, there.'

'What did he tell you about me?'

'Do you know him?'

'We met once. What did he tell you?'

Sunrise

3

Once I had the thread in my hands, I tried to unravel the ball to the end, pull everything out thread by thread, giving question after question. Of course, if it hadn't been for Revolver Mick's unexpected visit, I never would have found out the truth. She would have concocted fairy tales. Moreover, Dina was confused by the fact that I hadn't tried to get close to her during the night. It was as if she was taking revenge out on me by talking about it. She had undressed herself mentally in front of me, it seemed that the story about her fall provided her with delight. Yes, she said, I am, there's nothing to be surprised about. From the tick-tock robot to the boat dock shed. About what happened in the shed, I could only imagine, guess; she herself said that she had gone on a walk with a guy, this guy brought her to the shed, began to thrust himself on her using dirty tricks, turned out to be a sadist, a monster, then she ran, shock set in, she fell asleep, a crazy situation, then she told me her entire life, how she had been a lodger, lover and housemaid and how little those men had paid her. This overly candid spiritual undressing made me cautious, I didn't really want to believe that she had worked in a printing house. I questioned her. Why, while working at the printing house, did she not ask for help from the labour union, the local committee, the secretary of the party organisation, the party director, why? Apparently there wasn't a dormitory available, no one managed (or also didn't want) to help, so here she told in detail what the local committee chairman had said, what the secretary of the party organisation had said, what the others had said, that she has a registered domicile, so she should be living there, that everything would be fine, it would work itself out in the near future, but no one could tell when that near future would come, and I understood that she really had worked at a printing house.

Sunrise

4

I steered my small car out of the garage, and Dina got in the front seat next to me. After a ride of fifteen minutes we had gotten to the city's central district, and Dina asked me to stop at one of the buildings.

After waiting for ten minutes, she returned with a suitcase and a fur coat, placed her things in the backseat and asked to drive elsewhere. Where? To one more place. Apparently she had a few things there as well, she would gather everything together, in another place. She took about five minutes or so, returned with a sports bag, threw it next to the suitcase and fur coat and asked me to drive elsewhere. To yet one more place.

'Wait for me. I will be five minutes or so.'

I waited. When Dina disappeared through the entrance door, I turned around in my seat, checked the suitcase locks; they yielded easily under finger pressure. The suitcase wasn't locked. I opened it. I looked at its contents. There were dresses thrown here and there, a half dozen pieces of women's underwear, all dainty, expensive, and also two pairs of shoes. Three pornographic magazines had been thrown on top, published in Scandinavia. I closed the suitcase, clicking the locks. I took a look in her sports bag. It was also full of clothes: there were sweaters, cotton shirts, scarves, good and expensive things. Her wardrobe. My Croesus-like arrogance subsided considerably.

'He doesn't want to give me my dress back,' Dina complained.

He wasn't giving a dress back. A grey, rose, blue, green, red, yellow velvet dress? It would haunt her dreams her whole life.

'What kind of dress?'

'A summer dress. With a ruffle flounce hem. Made out of blue silk.'

'And you need it, right?'

'Very much so.'

'Alright,' I said, 'which flat is it?'

'Number seven.'

'Is he at home alone?'

'He's alone.'

I was certain that he had hidden the dress somewhere. In a safe place. How would I have acted if my wife returned, but my lover would have forgotten her dress? I would have hidden it in a safe place. Where could I find a safe place in his flat? In the pantry? – impossible. In a closet? – not there either, she would be rummaging around there too often. In the attic? – his wife could happen upon it by accident while hanging up the clothes to dry. In long boots? Behind the book shelf? In the piano, behind the paintings, in a box, but maybe in long boots?

'Do you have long boots?' I asked.

'What? What do you mean?'

'Long boots.'

'No, I don't.'

In the couch cushions? While cleaning them his wife could find it. It was doubtful it would be in the flat, so in the cellar then. In the wood cellar. However, there were zigzag-like central heating radiators underneath the windows, there was a tile stove, but they didn't heat it anymore. So – in the tile stove, if you thought about it, it was a safe place, the tile stove wasn't being heated, you had to wrap it up in stiff paper, bury it in the ashes, maybe he had to stick it in the chimney?

'Pull the dress out, it's in the stove,' I said.

'Ah. You're here for the dress? Who are you to Dina exactly?'

'It's not important. Pull the dress out.'

'Pull it out yourself.'

I went over to the tile stove, opened the little door with great effort, clink, clang. I peered into the shallow black mouth. I didn't see anything. I took a newspaper from the table, rolled it up, and poked around the ashes. I squatted, then bent over in a hook, and stuck my hand in the chimney. Nothing.

'I have another tile stove,' he said with a smirk. 'I haven't heated that one for a long time either.'

'Give me the dress,' I repeated angrily.

It's already an old stroke of bad luck. As soon as we get into a funny situation, we become angry.

'Alright, alright,' he said, yielding suddenly, 'I'll go get it. Sit down, wait a minute.'

I sat down on a rickety Viennese chair, and looked out through the window. I heard, behind me, in another room, the tile stove door was clinking, clink, clang, but I just looked out of the window, sitting on the rickety Viennese chair. Unexpectedly, I felt a sharp cold blade against my neck. About three fingers away from my ear, the cold, sharp, steely, and lightly shaking blade touched my neck from behind.

Sunrise

5

A squeaky little voice said:

'Don't move, otherwise it's over!'

A voice could be heard coming from the other room.

'Jānis, leave the man alone, what did I tell you!'

I turned around to look. A little blond boy with a sailor's cutlass had come in very quietly, then the boy laughed, look, look, how much the man was scared. Papa, the man was scared.

'Are you a little tick-tock robot?' I asked, grabbing him.

'That's me,' the boy responded.

'Here's the dress.' The father handed me a package. I noticed traces of ash in spots. 'Tell me, who are you to Dina?'

I bid him farewell by saying 'Goodbye,' in place of an answer. Dina was waiting for me in the car.

'Why didn't he give you the dress?' I asked.

'He wanted me to stay. His wife left him again.'

'Ah, I see. And why didn't you stay?'

She shrugged her shoulders. That meant – are you stupid?!

'Who's the boy? He's in that three-by-four photograph.'

'There's this boy. Maybe when we get married.'

We drove up to another house, and Dina brought her things there. It was there her girlfriend lived. Her girlfriend supposedly had a secure income, that's what Dina told me as we were driving, apparently there was a syndicate, a perfume shop, a customer would come, say the password, buy perfume for fifteen roubles, pay the money at the counter, wait while they pack it, and during that time

SHE would come, a high-class woman, a boa scarf, elegant clothing, beautiful, just a little too much make-up on, but that's the fashion around the world, the customer takes the perfume, takes HER, then leaves, but the perfume travels back to the shop, everything is done to the letter, honestly, within the boundaries of business, the law is not broken, the number of customers is very limited, mostly long-distance sailors, also a few land rats with big wallets, everything is kept well-secret, everyone is given the password. A nice girlfriend, Dina will be staying with her for a time now.

Occasionally I become uncomfortable from such openness. Dina speaks with me pragmatically like she's talking with a colleague of her trade. She was sure that she could trust me. Yes. Let everything flow past like clear, flowing water, let it run like a rabbit with light steps? Sooner or later we had to meet. The only framework in my life was work, the rest I let slip through my hands, I scattered it into the air, the rest was enjoyment for me. Living meant enjoying. Why not after all? Even in such a small detail, in walking across the street, I delighted in the roundness of the cobblestones under my feet, I was a hedonist, I created a demand, the demand created a supply, which is why Dina had to appear, the conditions were ripe for it, yes, the laws are cruel, as if all the abscesses had been treated, the illnesses treated, everything created for a harmonious life, our social incubator worked at full force, but the law, the iron law of supply and demand, well, see, it comes full circle, we have met. Work is the only thing that lifts me up, work is the only thing that I know, work is my only ship, during my holidays, while I was on dry land, we had to meet.

Everything there was to know about Dina – twenty years old, education – secondary, parents – elderly people somewhere far away in a rural area, height – average, well developed, around one metre and sixty-eight centimetres tall, hair colour – dark brown, natural hair colour hard to determine, it's possible it was greyish yellow, weight – around sixty kilogrammes, hotness scale, using a ten-point system – around eight and a half.

Sunrise

6

So, we were driving. She changed her clothes, sorted out her hair while she was in her girlfriend's flat, she asked me to wait for her, if I didn't have anything against it, could I take her for a drive. Where? Oh, it doesn't matter, let's go where you want. And so we went. We galloped at sixty-five kilometres an hour confined in that metal beetle (I couldn't squeeze more out of that engine), we drove out of the city, the city embraced us with its shabby arms of suburbs, as not all highways were flanked by new residential building districts.

Though I had only slept for a couple of hours, I felt great. The day had also turned out beautiful, with blue skies, green fields, a sweet-smelling spring day. The night's dark, velvety steps covered the continents and seas on the other side of the massive globe, and it seemed hard to believe that the night would once again come here, that once again it would switch on the stars, and switch on loneliness, maybe the night is a trap, a fateful trap, and I am driving at sixty-five kilometres an hour, the road is flashing by under the wheels, my house flashed under the wheels, the pots on the stove thundered, and a fight broke out on the ground floor, my first enemies, the master, the commander, the holy spirit, flashed under the wheels, I have to get up after so many long years, because otherwise I will live my life just as empty as I have until this moment and I won't have an excuse, over it, I drove over words, a foundling flashes under the wheels, carried through the centuries in the veiny palm of time, I sped over it at sixty-five kilometres an hour, I was darting forward quickly, a dying dog flashed under the wheels, and the stench of rotting flesh followed the car, a broken record flashed under the wheels, and the chord of a waltz rang out pitifully, a horse in the barn hanging from the rafters by its hind legs flashed under the wheels, its head cut off, its insides taken out, right at that moment they are skinning it, Mr Dārziņš's face and clean, proper suitcoat flashed by, clippity-clop, clippity-clop, the tanks are in our cities, Uncle Hans's grave flashed by, '*gut* boy' and '*gut* horse', shoobie doobie, you're my caraway seed bunny, a celestial mask, a tiny dormouse, I drove over them, clenching my teeth, and my heart is joyful, I drove over molten gold, I crossed over the scents of lavender and rosemary oils, cherry-red couches flashed under the wheels, my great love, the unfinished struggle flashed under the wheels, the student from a neighbouring house flashed, a brown clay bowl with the seminal glands, I drove over all of it at sixty-five kilometres an hour, the day had turned out fantastically, with blue skies, green fields, I myself flashed under the wheels of my car, the little airplane flashed, I galloped along the earth's cheek at sixty-five kilometres an hour (I wasn't able to squeeze more out of my engine), and next to me sat the beautiful Dina, retelling me the contents of a few films, oh, how they loved, how they cheated, conquered, surrendered themselves, sold themselves out, lived happily till the end of their lives, till the end of their long lives.

We turned off the main road. We drove through the forest. In the middle of a field there were bluish-grey ruins, we drove up and parked the car in the shade. We then went into the castle's inner courtyard. The walls had been preserved to some extent, the wind didn't blow there, the sun beat down on the long grass of the last year, the uncut grass, and in the old ruins of the castle, lying down in the grass of the last year, I attained Dina, the beautiful prostitute, the glimmering May sun shone over us, the new, green shoots of grass squeezed through the old grass of last year, it was dry, it was rustling, and I kissed Dina's face, lips, neck, I kissed her stomach, I attained her, there was silence all around, larks suspended themselves in the air like fine silver chime-bells, and in the corner of half-crumbling walls, lying in last year's grass, on my shabby raincoat I attained Dina, the beautiful prostitute, her breasts slid under my eager fingers, the smooth, white hemispheres, I kissed her pink nipples, in last year's grass within the old castle's gloomy walls, in a nest warmed by the sun, I did that.

Before we got into the car and drove back, I burned last year's grass in all four corners of the courtyard. The sun-baked dry grass caught fire quickly, and a moment later the entire courtyard was wriggling in the flames, in fire snakes, and we drove off, leaving a carpet of flames in place of struggles, blood, disgrace and servitude.

Sunrise

7

All of this happened to me, but for the moment I didn't know anything, I didn't know what would happen to me. Sitting in a deep, worn-out lounge chair, in which Mr. Dārziņš had so gladly sprawled out back in the old days, I was reading a book and smoking a pipe with pleasant-smelling tobacco. Although low temperatures had persisted for a few nights, the window facing the street was open, and my legs were pleasantly warmed by a soft camel-hair blanket. The hands of the enormous clock, the first a short, fat man just like Sancho Panza, the second a tall, slender, man exactly like Don Quixote, were approaching midnight.

Translator's acknowledgements

Behind any book is generally an army of people and institutions that deserve mention. I'd like to thank the Latvian Literature platform for the financial support, the Ventspils Writers and Translators House for a residency during where I began translating *Insomnia*, Vilis Kasims for the many conversations concerning the contents of the book, Diana Strausa for her sharp eye in editing much of the first draft of the translation, and the people at Parthian Books for taking on this monumental work. I'd especially like to thank the author for his guidance, willingness to answer my many questions, and support in translating this novel.

Parthian Books: Recommended Fiction

The Blue Tent
Richard Gwyn
ISBN 978-1-912681-28-0
£9.99 Paperback

'One of the most satisfying, engrossing and
perfectly realised novels of the year.'
– *The Western Mail*

"This book is itself a sort of portal, where the
novelist-as-alchemist builds us a house
in the hills and then fills it ... with a
convincing magic.'
– *Nation.Cymru*

'A mysterious, dream-like story, delicately-
written and with a disturbing undertow,
The Blue Tent is in the best tradition of
modern oneiric fiction.'
– Patrick McGuinness

The Levels
Helen Pendry
ISBN 978-1-912109-40-1
£8.99 Paperback

'...with all the tension and plot twists and
turns that you would expect from a gripping
crime novel, makes an unsettling,
compelling read.'
– *Morning Star*

'...this is an assured novel and marks Helen
Pendry as an important new literary voice.'
– Kirsti Bohata, *Wales Arts Review*

'This is an elegant, wise and warm story that
stays with you long after finishing it.'
– Mike Parker

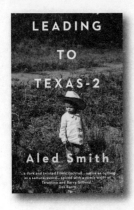

Leading to Texas-2
Aled Smith
ISBN 978-1-912109-11-1
£8.99 Paperback

'Aled Smith has mixed a dark and
twisted filmic cocktail.'
– Des Barry

Zero Hours on the Boulevard
ed. Alexandra Büchler
& Alison Evans
ISBN 978-1-912109-12-8
£8.99 Paperback

'A book about friendship, community,
identity and tribalism...'
– *New Welsh Reader*

Ironopolis
Glen James Brown
ISBN 978-1-912681-09-9
£9.99 Paperback

'The most accomplished working-class
novel of the last few years.'
– *Morning Star*

'...nothing short of a triumph.'
– *The Guardian*

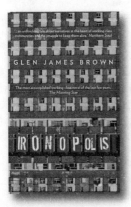

PARTHIAN

CARNIVALE

2 0 1 9 / 2 1

La Blanche
Maï-Do Hamisultane
Translated by Suzy Ceulan Hughes
ISBN 978-1-91-268123-5
£8.99 • Paperback

TRANSLATED BY JULIA AND PETER SHERWOOD
The Night Circus
and Other Stories
Uršuľa Kovalyk

TRANSLATED BY SUZY CEULAN HUGHES
La Blanche
Maï-Do Hamisultane

The Night Circus
and Other Stories
Uršuľa Kovalyk
Translated by Julia and
Peter Sherwood
ISBN 978-1-91-268104-4
£8.99 • Paperback

Fiction in Translation

The Book of Katerina
Auguste Corteau
Translated by Claire Papamichael
ISBN 978-1-91-268126-6
£8.99 • Paperback

TRANSLATED BY CLAIRE PAPAMICHAEL

The Book of Katerina
Auguste Corteau

'Filled with magical work, therapeutic, artistic... and playful. Playful about the woman who writes, about the woman who suffers...'
MIREN IBARLUZEA, *BIZKAIE*

A Glass Eye
Miren Agur Meabe

A Glass Eye
Miren Agur Meabe
Translated by Amaia Gabantxo
ISBN 978-1-91-210954-8
£8.99 • Paperback

Her Mother's Hands
Karmele Jaio

Translated by Kristin Addis
ISBN 978-1-91-210955-5
£8.99 • Paperback

WINNER
ENGLISH PEN
AWARD

WINNER
For Lady Plata Prize

WINNER
Zazpi Kale Prize

Seventh Igartza
Prize

'Jaio is undoubtedly a very skilful narrator'
IÑIGO ROQUE, *GARA*

Her Mother's Hands
Karmele Jaio

PARTHIAN
CARNIVALE
2019/21

PARTHIAN *Poetry in Translation*

Home on the Move
Two poems go on a journey
Edited by Manuela Perteghella
and Ricarda Vidal
ISBN 978-1-912681-46-4
£8.99 | Paperback
'One of the most inventive and necessary
poetry projects of recent years...'
– **Chris McCabe**

Pomegranate Garden
A selection of poems by Haydar Ergülen
Edited by Mel Kenne, Saliha Paker
and Caroline Stockford
ISBN 978-1-912681-42-6
£8.99 | Paperback
'A major poet who rises from [his] roots to touch
on what is human at its most stripped-down,
vulnerable and universal...'
– **Michel Cassir, *L'Harmattan***

Modern Bengali Poetry
Arunava Sinha
ISBN 978-1-912681-22-8
£11.99 | Paperback
This volume celebrates over one hundred years
of poetry from the two Bengals represented
by over fifty different poets.